Dreaming Dangerous

Also by Lauren DeStefano

A Curious Tale of the In-Between
The Peculiar Night of the Blue Heart
The Girl with the Ghost Machine

Dreaming Dangerous

Lauren DeStefano

BLOOMSBURY
CHILDREN'S BOOKS
NEW YORK LONDON OXFORD NEW DELHI SYDNEY

BLOOMSBURY CHILDREN'S BOOKS
Bloomsbury Publishing Inc., part of Bloomsbury Publishing Plc
1385 Broadway, New York, NY 10018

BLOOMSBURY and the Diana logo are trademarks of Bloomsbury Publishing Plc

First published in the United States of America in July 2018
by Bloomsbury Children's Books

Bloomsbury books may be purchased for business or promotional use. For information on
bulk purchases please contact Macmillan Corporate and Premium Sales Department at
specialmarkets@macmillan.com

Library of Congress Cataloging-in-Publication Data
Names: DeStefano, Lauren, author.
Title: Dreaming dangerous / by Lauren DeStefano.
Description: New York : Bloomsbury, 2018.
Summary: At Brassmere Academy for the Extraordinary, twelve-year-old Plum and her best
friends share adventures in dreams each night, but when Artem disappears they discover
alarming secrets about Brassmere and its intentions.
Identifiers: LCCN 2017034053 (print) • LCCN 2017049670 (e-book)
ISBN 978-1-68119-447-9 (hardcover) • ISBN 978-1-68119-448-6 (e-book)
Subjects: | CYAC: Best friends—Fiction. | Friendship—Fiction. | Dreams—Fiction. | Adventure
and adventurers—Fiction. | Ability—Fiction. | Schools—Fiction. | Orphans—Fiction. |
Supernatural—Fiction.
Classification: LCC PZ7.D47 Dre 2018 (print) | LCC PZ7.D47 (e-book) | DDC [Fic]—dc23
LC record available at https://lccn.loc.gov/2017034053

Book design by Jeanette Levy
Typeset by Westchester Publishing Services
Printed and bound in the U.S.A. by Berryville Graphics Inc., Berryville, Virginia
2 4 6 8 10 9 7 5 3

All papers used by Bloomsbury Publishing Plc are natural, recyclable
products made from wood grown in well-managed forests. The manufacturing processes
conform to the environmental regulations of the country of origin.

To find out more about our authors and books visit www.bloomsbury.com
and sign up for our newsletters.

Dreaming Dangerous

PROLOGUE

Off of Highway 305, between the winding loops and swirls of road and the sparkling city lights, there lies a forest. The forest is dark and thick—even in the winter, when most ordinary trees would be bare and dead.

Many years ago, a wealthy businessman by the name of Bartholomew Bartlesworth had planned to raze the forest and turn it into a super mall. For months there had been signs advertising it. The Greatest Mall Known to Man, the signs all read, accompanied by a drawing of a building so high that it disappeared into the clouds.

But before Bartholomew Bartlesworth could chop down even a single tree, he disappeared. Some say that he ran out of money. Some say he changed his mind. But most say that the forest ate him like a slice of delicious cake.

It wouldn't be the first time. Before Bartholomew Bartlesworth, the city zoning committee had attempted to build a bicycle path and a hiking trail, only to have the machines disappear by morning. It was a strange forest, and anyone with any sense would be wise to avoid it.

Some have said that the forest is filled with monsters. Others say the forest *is* the monster. But the truth, which very few people will ever know, is that the forest is protecting an important secret, and it does not take kindly to anyone who comes too close to discovering it.

CHAPTER 1

Brassmere Academy for the Extraordinary was surrounded by a tall iron fence whose poles were adorned with spikes. The fence had only one set of doors, which was guarded on either side by two stone gargoyles with twelve-inch fangs and gleaming silver talons. It was rumored that the gargoyles were alive, and that they would attack if they smelled blood they deemed suspicious.

The students at Brassmere always stayed inside the fence. There was no reason not to. The space inside the iron fence was the size of a small city. It had brick roads that all led back to Brassmere. There were lakes and waterfalls and hills, cafés, an arcade, and a library with a massive spiral staircase that went seven stories underground.

The only visitors came on every third Wednesday. Men and women in pink suits with white-and-brown-striped ties. They looked like walking, talking candy, the students thought. And sometimes they even brought some, if the students didn't complain or cry about having their blood drawn or their heartbeat recorded.

Plum had never cried—not even once in her twelve years. If the men and women in pink were to ask the students who among them was the bravest (and they sometimes did), the students who were being honest would say that it was Plum. She was also the fastest, and the highest climber, and the smoothest reader. And because of these attributes, some students adored Plum, while others had come to hate her.

When the men and women in pink arrived that Wednesday afternoon, it was raining heavily.

There were two hundred students exactly, all sitting in a row on a bench in a hallway that seemed to stretch on forever.

The students were talking quietly as they waited for their names to be called, their reports resting on their laps in white folders with the school's twin gargoyles emblazoned on the front in gold. Each time a student entered the closed door where the pink suits were waiting, the remaining students shuffled to the right, closing the empty space.

Plum was not nervous. She never was. Her dark hair was pulled into twin braids woven with shiny green ribbons. Normally she despised ribbons, but on report day she made an effort to be pristine.

To her left, Artem was fidgeting with his report, while beside him, Vien sat with perfect poise. Vien was the best at looking calm, whether or not he really was.

"They're taking a long time with Gwendle," Artem said.

Plum looked at the clock above the closed door. The hands were made of lacquered wood, carved into long, thin owls with menacing eyes. "It's only been five minutes," she said. "She'll have a lot to report. Our dreams have been much more dangerous lately."

Artem opened his mouth to say something, but the doorknob turned.

Gwendle stepped out into the hallway, the folder in her hand now empty after turning in her report. She gave Plum, Artem, and Vien a brief smile before she made the long walk down the hall.

A woman in pink came to the door and said, "Plum—yes, there you are. Hello."

Plum stood, adjusting the pleats of her maroon skirt.

The room at the end of the hall was always closed, except on the third Wednesday of each month, when the men and women in pink came to visit. Plum thought this was a shame, as it was such a pretty room, with oak chairs and plush white cushions, and a crystal chandelier that made the walls look like the reflection of water. There was a fireplace carved to look like the yawning mouth of a giant jungle cat whose tongue was made of flame and whose tail crept halfway up the wall.

There were only two pinks today, a man seated at one end of a grand table that could have seated every student at Brassmere, and the woman who'd greeted her at the door.

A pile of student reports were on the table as well.

"Please have a seat, Plum," the pink who'd greeted her at the door said. Plum sat at the head of the table, as was custom, and began rolling up the sleeve of her silver-and-white-striped blouse. They'd want to draw her blood. Blood always came first.

"How have you been since the last time I saw you, Plum?" asked the pink who was preparing the syringe. He had a kind face and warm brown eyes. Plum was glad he'd come this month; sometimes the pinks who drew blood were rough and impatient and left her with a bruise, but not this one. She hated when the syringes hurt, but more for Artem's sake than her own. He was especially sensitive to pain, and she didn't like it when any of her friends were upset.

"I've been well," Plum said. She watched as the needle sank into the vein in her forearm and the vial began filling with her blood.

The pink man smiled at her. "I'm sure you were very thorough in your report. We've just spoken to Gwendle, and she tells us you've been having dreams that are more disturbing than usual."

Plum considered this. "The monsters have been harder to kill," she said. After the syringe was withdrawn and a white bandage was placed on her arm, her wrist was fitted with a cuff that monitored her pulse. There was a wire leading from the cuff to a briefcase laid out on the table, filled with gears and circuits.

"Have you experienced anything strange upon waking up?" the pink woman asked.

"No," Plum said. She knew that concise answers were preferred. This was especially difficult for Artem, who rambled when he was nervous. The pinks always made him nervous.

"You're still close with your classmates Gwendle, Artem, and Vien, yes?" the pink woman asked. "Have you talked about anything unusual lately?"

"No," Plum said. This was a standard question, although she couldn't imagine what would be considered unusual. She had been dreaming in tandem with Gwendle, Artem, and Vien for as long as she could remember. Their entire friendship was centered around this unique bond the four of them shared. To someone on the outside of that bond, Plum supposed everything about them was unusual.

"Do you have many other friends, Plum?"

"Yes."

"Any enemies?"

Plum blinked. "Enemies?"

"Rivals." The pink woman tried that word instead.

"Jeremy can run nearly as fast as I can. Sometimes we make a game of competing. Vien keeps time for us."

"Would you say that Vien is your favorite friend?" the pink woman asked.

"Favorite?" Plum had never been asked such a thing. "No."

"And Artem? Gwendle? Are either of them your favorite?"

"I don't have a favorite," Plum said. She knew it was best not to give too much thought to these answers. Overthinking could change her pulse, and her pulse needed to be steady, so that the pinks would know that she was healthy.

"That will be all." The pink woman smiled.

"Go on and enjoy your day, Plum. I look forward to reading your report."

When Plum stepped out of the room, Artem was watching her. She smiled at him, and he seemed relieved. He did not like report day. He had a head for numbers and shapes and chemical reactions, but he struggled when it came to words. Reading them, but especially writing them. And reports were confidential, which meant that he couldn't ask Plum to read it back for errors.

She wanted to tell him not to worry, but speaking in the hallway after finishing a report meeting wasn't allowed.

She met Gwendle at the end of the long hallway, in the lobby away from the bench of students. Gwendle was sitting on the wide ledge of the massive stained-glass window, swinging her feet. Her yellow hair reflected the gray gloom of the rainy day. "So?" she said when Plum hopped up beside her. "How was it? Did they ask you about our dreams?"

"Not very much," Plum said.

"My report was a wild one this time, that's for sure," Gwendle said. "Half of it was about the Red Dragon. The one that tore Artem's arm off."

That dream had felt especially real. For days after, Artem rubbed at his arm as though it really had been torn off by the teeth of a murderous dragon and then stitched back on.

"I wrote about it, too," Plum said. Now that their reports were turned in, there was no harm talking about them. "And the river castle that had no doors."

"I hope we dream that one again," Gwendle said. "I'd like to find a way inside."

Plum laughed. "Don't let Artem hear you say that. He thinks it's full of bees."

"He is such a scaredy-cat," Gwendle said. "It's only a dream. Even if there were bees, they can't really hurt us."

By the time Artem and Vien were through handing in their reports, the rain had turned into a light drizzle.

"I'm starved," Gwendle said. "Lunch?"

"Definitely," Vien said.

They each grabbed a silver umbrella from the collection of them hanging along the foyer like sleeping bats, and they headed to their favorite café, #3.

Their untroubled expressions made Plum think they hadn't been asked anything strange. Was she the only one who had been asked if she had a favorite? It seemed like an absurd idea. She had known the three of them for as long as she could remember. They were friends, but something even stronger than ordinary friends, because they shared everything—even their dreams.

Everyone at Brassmere could do something extraordinary. Melinda, Trina, James, and Clayton could bend and move metal if they concentrated. Blare and Hutch could charm animals. The triplets, Sadie, Selene, and Sasha, could communicate with their thoughts; they were also Brassmere's only siblings and absolutely identical, which was enough to make them fascinating even among the exceptional.

The list of talents went on and on: breathing underwater, levitating, learning an entire language after hearing just one word of it.

The students at Brassmere understood that ordinary people did not have talents, but with the exception of their teachers and servers and the men and women in pink, they had no idea what an ordinary person would be like. To them, extraordinary *was* ordinary.

Sometimes, Plum wondered if her parents had been ordinary. Wondering about her parents was the only secret she kept from her friends and the only thing she never included in her reports. None of the students at Brassmere had parents. In addition to being extraordinary children, they were also orphaned, or abandoned. Sole survivors of accidents or illnesses, or found as crying infants on church steps and in alleyways.

The world outside Brassmere was a very dangerous place from what Plum had been told.

In her lessons, Plum had learned that the world was very big and filled with people. But so few of them were extraordinary, and those were the ones that Dr. Abarrane had rescued and brought here. They were lucky. Chosen by hand.

Over sandwiches and fizzing sodas topped with globs of whipped cream, Plum, Artem, Gwendle, and Vien talked about the Red Dragon. Artem began rubbing at his shoulder.

"It's been in four dreams, and we still haven't killed it," Plum said.

"It keeps killing us," Vien said.

Plum took a sip from her soda straw, watching him, considering the pink woman's question about Vien being her favorite. "That was a strange thing to ask," Plum thought. She was not one to dwell on things, but just this once, she couldn't help it. Vien was more in focus today, as though someone had shone a spotlight over him, rendering the world around him dull.

He had straight hair just long enough to tuck behind his ears. At a glance it was black, but when Plum stared at it, she could see hints of blue and gray where the light hit it. His eyes matched; on bright days, his black eyes turned warm brown in beams of sunlight. There was a divot between his eyebrows that deepened when he was thinking.

He was thinking now, as he tried to come up with an answer for the Red Dragon's behavior. Plum didn't hear whatever it was he said.

"Hey." Gwendle's bubbly voice snapped Plum out of her thoughts. "Are you okay?"

"Hm?" Plum blinked. "Oh. Yes." Her cheeks felt strangely warm.

Artem looked concerned. "Did the pinks take too much blood from you?"

"That's never happened," Plum said. Left

unchecked, Artem would spiral into worries about things that would not—that *could not*—ever happen. It was best to correct him before his imagination went too far. She took a bite from her sandwich, as though to emphasize her point. Blackberry jam bled out between the crusts. "The pinks always know what they're doing."

"Maybe not *always*," Vien said. His voice was low, and he twirled his straw between his thumb and index finger.

Gwendle's eyes were wide. "What do you mean?" she whispered.

Artem shifted uncomfortably in his chair. Questioning the pinks was insubordination. Any student who questioned a figure of authority at Brassmere was dealt with privately by Dr. Abarrane. It was the duty of any student who witnessed a student being insubordinate to report it. But the bond that Plum, Gwendle, Artem, and Vien shared defied that. It was unspoken, and yet they all knew that they existed in a world of their own, with its own rules, its own loyalties.

"Haven't you noticed?" Vien met Plum's eyes and held her gaze for a moment before he looked to the others. "Haven't the questions lately been strange for all of you, too?"

"Not for me," Gwendle said.

"I don't think so," Artem said.

But Plum didn't answer, and she felt three pairs of eyes studying her, waiting. She looked at Vien. In the gloomy rainy light that came through the windows, his eyes were black and deep.

He always seemed to know what she was thinking, Plum thought. Maybe she didn't have to give him an answer. Maybe he already knew what the pinks had asked her. Maybe he already knew that she was starting to wonder if she had lied when she gave her answer.

She was grateful that the pinks were not here now to monitor her pulse. There were no machines to betray the sincerity of her words.

Still, she chose her words carefully. There were students all around them, and it was impossible to know who might be listening.

"We aren't little kids anymore," Plum said. "Our instructors did tell us the questions would change as we got older." Their class was the oldest of all the students at Brassmere. They charted the path for the younger students, and there were no older students to tell them what to expect.

"We've already experienced things changing, haven't we?" Plum went on. "Our dreams are stronger. We die more often because we're still not as strong as the things we're fighting."

"Maybe." Vien's voice trailed. He didn't sound convinced, and Plum had a sinking feeling in her stomach that she had let him down. She wanted to ask him what the pinks had said during his meeting. She wanted to say, "Yes, things *are* strange. Maybe the pinks *don't* know everything." But she said nothing of the sort. Of course she didn't.

There were some things best left unsaid.

The rain turned to thunder. The loud, roaring sort of thunder that shook the ground and seemed to rattle the tree branches.

They ran from the café and down the cobblestoned path, and Artem was the one to pull them toward the arcade, which was much closer than the dormitories and would offer shelter from the rain.

"You hate the arcade," Gwendle said, once they'd stepped inside. "You say it's too loud." She wrung the water from her hair.

"I don't care to be struck by lightning, either," Artem said. "That takes precedence." "Precedence" was one of his favorite words ever since he'd learned it last year. He always said it with a confident air, as though he felt brilliant to know such an important word.

"Oh, come on." Gwendle clapped a hand to his shoulder. "The odds of being hit by lightning are nearly impossible."

Normally Artem would have an argument for

this, but today he just shrugged and walked on ahead.

The arcade was four stories high, and as Artem often lamented, it was quite noisy. It was meant to be a reward for students who worked hard and excelled in their academics. Only students whose grades and fitness performance were floundering were denied access until they improved, as a means to motivate them.

The main floor of the arcade had bright green carpeting and several game stations. There were cars stationed before screens with simulated roads, electric basketball hoops that flashed with color when a basket was made, and several games that involved dancing—some with a partner and some without.

The music from each game blended and blurred into a cacophony.

To the far end, beside a giant machine that popped fresh popcorn and kept it warm, there was a row of tables and a shelf of old board games whose boxes were discolored and held together by bits of tape. They were no match for the intrigue and allure of bright lights and catchy music, and that was precisely why Artem liked them.

The four of them assembled around a table, out of the glow of most of the arcade games, but not at all immune to their noise.

Vien selected one of his favorite games, which of course involved logic and strategy and contemplation, and Artem set about arranging the pieces.

Gwendle rested her chin on her palms and sighed, as though to say she was bored. She didn't much care for quiet games. She excelled at dancing and sharpshooting virtual discs on one of the arcade screens. But she didn't voice her displeasure because it was clear that something was troubling Artem.

After the pieces were laid out, Artem finally spoke. His voice was soft, and they all had to strain to hear him over the games.

 22

"Do you ever wonder about the pinks?" he asked.

"What do you mean?" Plum asked, setting her pawn on the board. Its shiny plastic reflected the bright lights on the ceiling.

Artem shrugged. He looked uneasy. "I mean, do you ever wonder what they do with our blood and our interviews? Where they go when they leave here."

"There's no mystery to that at all. They test our blood to make sure we're healthy," Gwendle answered brightly. "There's nothing strange about it, and the needle barely even hurts."

"But what is it all for?" Artem pressed. "Why did Dr. Abarrane bring us here?"

Vien's expression turned thoughtful, then concerned. "Why are you asking about these things?"

"There has to be a purpose, doesn't there?" Artem said. "We're the oldest class at Brassmere. What happens when we're older? Will we work here?"

"I might," Gwendle said. "I've always liked the idea of being a teacher."

Artem looked to Plum, his eyes pleading. "What about you?" he said. "Do you ever wonder what's outside? Where the pinks are going when they leave?"

Plum blinked. "It's dangerous out there, Artem," she said. "Maybe Dr. Abarrane is preparing us for that. If we're meant to know, we'll know."

"Real-life monsters?" Artem's tone was cynical. "Is that it?"

"We don't know what Dr. Abarrane's plan for us is," Vien agreed. "But he'll make sure we know when it's time."

Artem slid his piece across the board, and he bowed his head. He didn't say anything more about it.

CHAPTER 2

Plum, Vien, Artem, and Gwendle had chosen one another. Dr. Abarrane liked to tell them this, and it was true. They had been at Brassmere since they were babies, and possibly had been sharing dreams even then—though there was no way to be certain.

Plum was the first of them who learned to crawl, and she'd made her way to Gwendle in the playroom. Vien was next, followed by Artem. When one of them cried, they all seemed to share in that distress. Every nanny at Brassmere had made a note of it. Over the years, Dr. Abarrane tested the power of their bond. He would assign them dormitories on opposite ends of the academy and make sure they didn't attend the same lessons. They would go days without communicating, and sometimes even weeks.

It didn't matter. They always met up again in their dreams. They never needed any guidance or instruction to find one another. It just seemed to happen.

At first, the dreams had been pleasant. Plum remembered this, though it was a fuzzy, faraway sort of memory of swing sets and swimming, sun and laughter.

The first monster had been a shadow that looked like a man in an overcoat and top hat, but who morphed into a dragon when it came close. They had been eight. Plum remembered this because the dream happened on the night of her birthday. It wasn't her real birthday—she couldn't know for certain when exactly she'd been born.

But it was the anniversary of the day Dr. Abarrane had found her.

They hadn't been frightened of the dragon at first. Nothing in their young lives had given them cause to be frightened at all. But then the dragon grabbed Artem in its talons and flew away with him.

It had taken what felt like hours to find him, after climbing through mountains as high as the clouds, hiking through shadows as dark as night.

Artem had been horribly frightened. Vien had been thoughtful, Gwendle curious. But Plum had resolved to be stronger. She took to the library that following afternoon and studied every detail about swords so that she might dream up a weapon worthy of slaying the next monster that dared to invade their dreams.

This proved to be useful, because the monsters soon became a regular occurrence.

Tonight, the dream began in a cave, and the cave was unfamiliar.

Plum was the first to arrive, which was typical. Gwendle kept a flashlight under her mattress—contraband—so that she could burrow herself under the blankets and stay up late to sketch. Artem was a fitful sleeper, and it took him the longest to settle into his dream state.

As for Vien, his mind liked to wander. Of the four of them, he was the only one to have solo dreams. He might be flying over burning cities or swimming into the mouth of a whale right about now. One could never be too certain.

Alone in the cave, Plum shivered. She could see her breath, and when she inspected her hands, fine icy lines traced her skin in snowflake shapes. She caught her reflection in a gleaming frozen stalactite and saw that blue circles traced her dark eyes.

She was wearing her school-issue nightshirt—red with the gold gargoyle logo across the stomach, with a hem that stopped midway down her calves.

A coat was too much to hope for in this place, she supposed. Dreaming up frivolous things like clothing was often a challenge. Dreaming up food was a specialty of Gwendle in particular. But Plum often found that she could not conjure the things she needed or wanted, even with the power of her will. She had learned to save her energy for what was most important, like weapons, which she would surely need in almost every dream. Monsters were a common occurrence.

She attempted to untie her braids, hoping her long hair would serve as a scarf. The ribbons wouldn't come undone, though, and she trudged forward, hugging her chest and rubbing her arms.

The cave was narrow, lit by faintly glimmering bits of purple and blue within the stone. Darkness awaited her at either direction, and as she walked, her bare feet made gentle splashing sounds against the wet earth.

"Gwendle?" she tried. "Artem? Vien?"

A grumble answered her—a low, inhuman creaking sound that could be mistaken for a dying man's laugh.

The walls began to shake.

Plum spun, rock crumbles falling down around her.

The grumble turned into a hiss. Plum reached over her head and broke the stalactite from the cave's ceiling. Immediately it transformed into her familiar sword, arched and gleaming. She bent her right knee, assuming her fighting stance.

But no monster emerged. The hiss turned to laughter, and then a voice spoke, clear as any waking sound. "Would you say that Vien is your favorite friend?"

The pink woman's voice.

Plum clutched her sword tighter, but a cold sweat formed at the nape of her neck.

A dragon, she had been prepared for. Or the rotted, staggering corpses of people she knew in life, freshly emerged from their graves. She knew a great bit about monsters and tricks. She would even have expected the darkness to swell and then burst into millions of bees.

But she had not expected this. Her eyes narrowed. "Who are you?"

Someone was there. She knew it.

The cave continued to shake, until the walls fell away and the ground dropped below Plum's feet. She was falling, falling.

Sword pointed downward, Plum leaned into the momentum of the drop, landing hard on her feet on the head of some giant, scaled creature. An alligator, she suspected. She jammed her sword between its eyes and it thrashed and roared.

Above her, stars began to emerge in the sky, and the stars were voices, asking questions in the pink woman's voice.

Blood stained her sword and her shoes. She was breathing hard, and her heart was racing.

The giant alligator would not die quickly. It

thrashed and bucked, trying to throw her into the foggy marsh upon which it floated. Plum drove her sword hilt in deeper.

Growls and snapping jaws told her that this was not the only creature she would have to defeat, though, and before she could react, a set of sharp teeth had snared her ankle and pulled her underwater.

Pay attention, Plum told herself as the air escaped her. *It's only a dream. Just a dream.*

Her lungs burned in protest. It was impossible to see at first, and then hazy swirls of red floated up before her eyes. She tasted the copper of blood. Her blood. The creature still had her ankle, and it was pulling her farther and farther from the surface.

Frantically she felt along her hips, hoping for some sort of weapon to appear in its hilt. There was always a weapon hidden somewhere. But all she felt was the fabric of her nightshirt.

She fumbled in the darkness, feeling the

monstrous alligator's face, searching for a weapon. *Come on, come on.* There had to be something she could fight with. But there was nothing. Her head was starting to feel light, her body numb. She hoped that she was waking, but knew how unlikely it was for a dream to end so soon.

Pay attention, she told herself again. There had to be a way out of this.

Something reached through the murk and the blood and pulled at her. They were hands, she realized, trying to free her. The monster, though, would not relent. It clamped on her leg until she could feel its teeth grating against bone.

Plum was too weak to scream. All she could think about was air. A great, open blue sky filled with it. When she came out of this, she would never ever take a breath for granted again.

Something darted past her. A cloud of black hair, then the flash of a jagged knife. *Vien.*

More blood bloomed like wildflowers in the water, but this time the blood did not belong to

Plum, and suddenly she was free. Someone was pulling her up, up, up.

Plum broke the surface with a gasp, and it felt as though her chest were ripping apart.

"It's okay." Gwendle's voice. "I've got you."

Gwendle had her arms burrowed under Plum's, and Plum sagged gratefully against her, taking a moment to collect herself.

"Thank you," she said at last.

Vien bobbed to the surface next, spluttering, his face dripping with pink bloody water. He paddled his way to Plum. The divot was prominent between his eyebrows as he studied her. "Are you all right?"

Plum's teeth were chattering. "My leg should heal itself in a moment."

"Moment" was their only measure of time when they were dreaming. Minutes and seconds and hours and even years all held their own meaning in dreams and were not to be trusted.

Gwendle whistled sharply, and something

swam toward them in the waters. It was not the drab green of the strange alligators, but rather a bright teal blue, like the paint in the girls' bathroom at Brassmere.

The creature was gigantic, and it swam under them and then began to surface, acting as a sort of island to protect them.

Plum sat on the creature's slick back, working the air back into her lungs. Vien fretted over her leg, which was mangled and red.

Gwendle set about the task of charming the creature that had rescued them. "There, there," she cooed, her voice turning into a little song. "You're a friend, aren't you? And you're so beautiful." It was some sort of whale that let out the cheerful whinnying of a horse when Gwendle lay on her stomach and petted it. Though she had a talent for throwing knives and possessed bizarre strength in her dream state, Gwendle's real weapons came in the form of animals. They were drawn to her, and eager to please her whims and fancies. Which was odd, given that animals avoided her when she was awake. The occasional stray cat that was sly enough to slip through the fence would hiss when she approached. Snakes flicked their tongues. Even mosquitoes wouldn't bother to suck her blood.

But as with many creatures in their dreams, this whale adored Gwendle as she hummed to it. The top of its tail flicked happily, and its lids were heavy as the effects of Gwendle's calming presence washed over it. It let out a sigh through its flared nostrils that rippled the water's surface.

"Take us to Artem," Gwendle said, and the whale began to coast forward.

"Where *is* Artem?" Plum asked. Vien shared a bunk with him and would have been the last to see him before he fell asleep.

"I thought he fell asleep first," Vien said. He had torn away his sleeve and was using it to wrap Plum's wound. "Does this hurt?"

Plum shook her head. Pain was fleeting here.

Still, when she looked down at the wound, she saw a dark patch of blood staining the makeshift bandage. Strange that it hadn't healed yet.

As the blue whale coasted forward, the sky began to shift from starry black to bright pink, and then the soft blue of dawn. It was comforting, the calm and the lull that happened either after something frightening, before something frightening, or in between frightening things.

Plum studied her hips, which were absent their familiar sheaths, wondering why this dream had not equipped her with her usual weapons. "If the alligator had eaten me, I would have woken up," she said. "Before either of you even got here."

"It would have been a solo dream," Gwendle said cheerily. She was patting the whale affectionately. Its massive body thrummed with a soft coo.

Plum puckered her mouth and considered this. What would a solo dream mean? She supposed it would be scary to have to face the monsters alone. Then again, none of the other students at Brassmere seemed afraid of their dreams. Perhaps monsters were less common in solo dreams. Perhaps solo dreams did not teach one to be brave or strong in the physical sense. Perhaps for some they were a place to reflect.

Tilly, a tall girl with dark eyes and freckles who was especially good at archery, had once told Plum that her own dreams were mostly a distorted version of what her day had been like, and what she expected of the days to come. They were often absurd, but rarely anything frightening.

A flock of birds fluttered overhead, and Plum turned her head to look. They were bright purple, with white-speckled wings.

"Artem must be nearby," Vien said, as the three of them looked up. Artem was always dreaming of things that could fly.

As though Vien's words made it true, Artem appeared through the haze that swirled over the water. There was an island just ahead of them now, its grass aggressively bright. Artem knelt near the shore, his eyes fixed on something that couldn't be seen from where they coasted.

"Where have you *been*?" Gwendle called out. The whale was swimming faster now, bringing them closer. "A giant alligator was eating Plum. We could have used your gills." Artem didn't really have gills, but in dreams he could always breathe underwater.

Artem didn't look up, and as the whale brought them to the water's edge, Plum's stomach filled up with dread. She looked to her leg, which had begun to hurt, and which was now bleeding through its bandage.

She was the first to stand, and the first to step onto the island. The grass doubled in height the moment her feet touched it, and continued to grow until it reached her shoulders. Artem, who had just been kneeling right in front of her, was far away now.

Plum heard Vien and Gwendle calling for her, but when she spun around, they were buried somewhere in the tall grass as well.

"I'm here." Artem's voice was a whisper in her ear. "Just ahead."

She moved forward, her heart beating faster now. Adrenaline made wounds bleed more, and Plum wished she hadn't learned this in her medicine courses, because now this always happened in her dreams. Her leg left a trail of blood behind her as she went.

There are no animals to hunt us here, she thought, willing it to be so. Sometimes this worked.

She found Artem in a small clearing, knelt over a lump of what appeared to be blankets.

Plum crouched across from him, the bundle lying between them. "What is it?" she asked.

Artem raised his head. In the shadow of the high grass, his face was pale. Dark blue circles ringed his eyes.

"They're coming for us." His voice was hollow and strange. "One by one, until they find the one they need."

"What are you talking about?" Plum's voice came out a hoarse whisper. Artem seemed in a trance, as though he were asleep even in his dream. "Who's coming for us?"

In answer, he ripped the blanket away, and when Plum looked at what lay between them, she saw herself. She saw herself still and white, with her arms crossed over her chest. Dead.

CHAPTER 3

Plum awoke with a gasp. Across the room, Gwendle stirred in her bed and then fell silent. The space between their beds felt impossibly vast. A canyon of wooden planks and a throw rug that was fraying at the edges.

The pendulum of the grandfather clock swung steadily, its brass face gleaming in a strip of moonlight.

For a few seconds, Plum didn't believe that she was awake at all. Dreams could be deceptive sometimes, and she looked for anything out of place. Faces in the shadows, or a metallic gleam to the spider that was dripping from the ceiling on a slender thread. She concentrated hard on these things. When she was awake, she always made a point of studying her surroundings so that she would be able to spot the discrepancies in convincing dreams, and because of this, she was never fooled.

Everything seemed real. She reached under her pillow for her leather-bound journal. It was exactly where she'd left it.

They're coming for us, she wrote, her eyes straining in the darkness. She pressed her fingertips to her throat and used the ticking of the pendulum to monitor her pulse, her breaths per minute. She recorded all her vitals and details of her dream, just in case anything escaped her the more time she spent in the waking world. Her final note read:

Startled awake for the first time.

She slid the lock into place on her journal

when she was done, sealing it with the key that always hung around her neck, and then she lay back down.

Professor Nayamor would want to know about this. Her star pupil, fit and fearless, being startled awake as though nightmares were a thing that rattled her. She had heard of children being startled awake by their nightmares before, of course, but she had never understood why a dream would be frightening when it had no true power to hurt the dreamer.

Though, this never seemed to reassure Artem.

She would of course have to write a full report in her journal, as she always did, especially when things were strange.

Sleep didn't come, no matter how still and quiet Plum lay waiting for it. By morning, when the dormitory began to fill with the sleepy glow of dawn's light, Plum was uneasy. Gwendle was still sleeping, quiet and calm, but something wasn't right about any of this.

At six o'clock exactly, the alarm on Gwendle's nightstand trilled out its pleasant but aggressively loud melody.

Gwendle's arm reached out from its pile of blankets to silence it.

Plum sat up for the first time in hours. Across the room, Gwendle did the same; her fine blond hair formed a static halo around her head. But she wasn't wearing her usual sleepy, cheerful face. She didn't say "good morning" or reach under her pillow for her journal.

Instead, she blinked at Plum, her face puzzled. "You were gone last night. You wandered off into the tall grass, and then we couldn't find you."

Plum glanced to the closed door of their tiny dormitory. It was a heavy, dark oak that muffled sounds, but even so, Plum felt that someone might be on the other side of it, listening.

She moved across the room and sat on Gwendle's bed. They crossed their legs and scooted closer to each other.

"What happened after I was gone?" Plum's voice was a whisper.

Gwendle squinted as she tried to remember. "I found Vien in the grass. It kept growing taller and taller until it blocked out the sun. We tried to find you and Artem, but the grass became heavy, until we couldn't push it out of our way."

"And then what?" Plum asked.

Gwendle blinked. "I don't remember." The words seemed to frighten her as soon as she'd said them. "I've never not remembered a dream before." She lifted her pillow, but before she could reach for her dream journal, Plum grabbed her wrist.

"Don't," she said.

"Don't?" Gwendle asked. "I have to. We have to write everything down. It's the rule."

"Something strange happened last night," Plum said. "We should talk to Artem and Vien before we do anything."

Gwendle hesitated, but then she put her pillow back in place.

As they got ready for their morning, Plum retrieved her own journal and laid it open on her mattress. With great care and precision, she tore her page of notes from the binding.

An hour later, when the breakfast bell chimed through the speakers, Plum was beginning to feel sleepy. She stared at her reflection in the mirror that hung on the wall over her dresser and made sure that the pleats of her skirt were sharp and that her hair was combed. Dark circles were appearing under her eyes, but they were hidden when she smiled.

She made a note to smile as much as possible today.

"Ready?" Gwendle asked. She looked prepared, as always. Even the papers in her folder were neatly arranged so that none of their corners peeked out.

"Yes," Plum said, and smiled.

Artem and Vien were waiting for them at the breakfast buffet. Vien looked well rested, Plum thought, but Artem seemed tired. He also had bags under his eyes, and even his brown hair seemed limp and wilted against the sides of his face.

Plum had no appetite, but she assembled fruit and toast neatly onto her plate. Vien was beside her now, and she heard the concern in his voice when he whispered, "What happened last night?"

Plum shook her head. Across the room, Professor Nayamor stood in her starched uniform, observing the children as she always did. Plum straightened her spine. "I don't know," she whispered back.

When the four of them sat at their usual table, they leaned close to one another. "What did you write in your journals this morning?" Gwendle asked, her eyes wide.

Artem and Vien looked at each other, hesitant. "We didn't," Vien answered. "We wanted to wait until all of us spoke."

"We didn't write anything, either," Plum

said, and she found herself grateful that Vien's practicality once again matched her own. She didn't bother to tell them about the notes she'd torn from her journal that morning. They were gone now; on her way to breakfast she fed them into the fireplace that burned in the dormitory's foyer.

"Let's compare what we remember," Vien said. As he went on, his story was very similar to Gwendle's: he lost Plum and Artem in the tall grass and never found either of them again.

"I woke up after that," Artem said.

"Me too." Plum squinted, pondering. "And you couldn't get back to sleep either, could you?"

"No." Artem's expression turned nervous. "We should tell Professor Nayamor. What if it means something bad?"

"It's only dreaming," Gwendle reminded him. "We've all lost legs and fingers and woken up just fine."

"Your leg was injured last night," Vien said to

Plum. "We couldn't get the bleeding to stop even once we were safe. That was new."

"It's better now," Plum said. "A dream injury can't hurt us."

"Do you remember what happened after we lost Plum and Artem?" Gwendle said.

Vien shook his head.

"We have to write *something* in our journals," Artem insisted. "Otherwise it will look too suspicious. What if there's an inspection?" Inspections were frequent, and never announced in advance. Students were never given time to prepare; otherwise their instructors would have no way of knowing if they were being genuine.

They spent the rest of their breakfast agreeing on a dream. They kept the alligators, but embellished on the details. It was not the first time that the four of them had ever conspired, but it was the first time they'd ever conspired to lie. The ease of the lie frightened them just a bit—the way it all came to them as easily as truth, the way their conscience didn't feel one bit bothered although to lie about their talents was the biggest crime a Brassmere student could commit.

It just felt right somehow, in a way that none of them could explain. Not that any of them tried to.

CHAPTER 4

Plum heard the music while she was staring up at the half-moon through her window. It was nearing midnight, and she had yet to fall asleep. Gwendle had nodded off hours ago, her cheek pressed against her sketchbook. The flashlight in her hand had long since died and gone dark.

It wasn't like her to be so late. Plum was known for her punctuality, and surely her friends were wondering what was taking so long. Gwendle might try to wake up and check on her, but waking from a tandem dream was no easy task.

They often felt themselves fading from their shared dream at the same time. One would disappear, then the next, and the next, as though they had planned it that way. Their recorded waking times were usually within one to two minutes of one another's.

Plum thought about this as she lay trying to return to her dream. They were so in sync, the four of them. So very different and yet so tightly connected, like strands in a braid forming a rope.

The music broke through what had been hours of silence, and Plum held her breath to listen for it. To call it music at all was generous. First there was one high note of a piano, then another, then a crash of keys, as though a herd of raccoons had crashed through the ceiling and landed on the piano.

It was coming from the grand foyer.

Plum climbed out of bed, curious. She counted the ticking of the clock, and noted the shadow of the skeletal tree painted against the wall, taking in all the details of reality to be sure this wasn't a dream. Things had felt very strange all day, and even with her reminders, she didn't feel certain that any of this was real.

The heavy oak door of her dormitory creaked as she pushed it open. The hallway was dark, all its dozens of doors closed. Plum heard someone's gentle snoring, but otherwise all was still.

Then, more piano keys being played, absent any rhythm.

She followed the sound to the grand foyer, which was also dark. But the moonlight spilled in through the high, arched windows, painting everything a ghostly blue.

Melinda stood over the piano in the grand foyer, in her red Brassmere nightshirt. Her fists were clenched at either side, and her eyes were a vacant, hollow gray. Her pupils were all but gone.

There were four students at Brassmere who could bend metal, but Melinda was easily the strongest among them, and the only one with enough concentration to bend piano strings.

Plum kept to the shadows as she approached, watching.

Melinda's hair was messy, as though she'd been sleeping. Her skin was paler than usual. Her expressionless face was pointed at the piano as one clumsy note preceded another.

Then, all at once, a song began to play. It was frenzied and beautiful and unlike anything Plum had ever heard. Her skin swelled with goose bumps.

The song went on for several seconds, until Plum was sure that it would wake everyone in the dormitory.

But as the song went on, none of the doors opened. Not even Professor Lillyn, who slept in the room at the end of the hall, came to check on the commotion.

Plum moved closer. The song ended, and the silence was startling. "Melinda?" Plum said. She was careful not to make any sudden moves. She had heard that it was dangerous to frighten someone if they were sleepwalking, and it was apparent now that Melinda was not awake.

Melinda raised her head. She looked through Plum, and then she looked right at her. It was a piercing gaze.

"They're coming for us," she said. Plum's blood went cold. It was the same thing Artem had said to her in their dream.

They're coming for us. Melinda's eyes were big and earnest now.

Plum knew that she was not dreaming. She looked at the windows that made up the entirety of the southernmost wall to be sure. Far beyond the trees, she could just make out the spiked tips of the iron fence that surrounded Brassmere. This was one of her reality points. There were never fences in any of her dreams.

She looked back at Melinda, steeling herself. There was nothing to be afraid of, she reasoned, and fear was useless, anyway. She told Artem this all the time. "Who is coming?" she asked.

Melinda pursed her lips, and it looked as though she was going to speak. But then a look of fear washed across her face and she gasped. A line of blood dripped from one of her nostrils. She wiped at it with one hand and stared at the red smear on her fingers.

Plum recognized the look on her face. It was fear. Melinda's pupils expanded, and she drew in a breath.

"Don't," Plum started to say. But it was too late. Melinda was already screaming.

Doors opened and footsteps creaked against the boards. Plum stepped backward into the crowd, immediately blending in with the rush of students who had just been roused from their sleep.

Professor Lillyn was running toward Melinda now, shouting directives to the children, saying, "Out of the way, file up against the wall."

If Melinda hadn't been awake moments

earlier, she certainly was now. She looked up at the foyer full of classmates, her eyes round and startled. She didn't know how she had gotten there, and probably didn't realize that the blood was just a nosebleed.

"All right, all right." Professor Lillyn drew the bench from the piano and guided Melinda to sit so that she could inspect the damage. "Are you hurt? Let me see your hands."

"Plum," Vien whispered. He was standing beside her now. "What happened?"

Students were crowded all around them, all eyes on Melinda and Professor Lillyn. Bloodshed wasn't uncommon at Brassmere, between the rope burns and skinned knees on the training courses, and soon everyone would realize that a bloody nose was hardly worth staying awake for.

Plum craned her neck and made sure nobody was paying her any mind. "Come on," she said, and led him down the hall and back to her room.

Gwendle's bed was empty and the room was

quiet, save for the ticking of the clock. Plum closed the door.

"Plum?" Vien said. "What is it? What happened?"

She stood close to him, so that she could make out the details of his face in the moonlight. "This is real, isn't it?" she said. "We aren't dreaming, are we?"

Vien inspected himself, and then his eyes did a sweep of the room, analyzing the details just as they'd been trained to.

"It doesn't feel like a dream to me," he said, and Plum felt some reassurance at that. He was never wrong about things like this.

"Something is happening," Plum said. "I don't know what it is yet, but I think something is trying to warn me."

Vien furrowed his brow. "What do you mean?"

"I sensed it in my dream last night. Artem was trying to warn me. He said that someone was coming. And then this morning he didn't remember any of it. Just now, the same thing happened to Melinda. She looked right at me and said, 'They're coming for us.'"

"'They,'" Vien echoed. "Who is 'they'?"

"I don't know yet." Plum gnawed her lip, something she hadn't done since she was very small, back when she still used to get nervous about things.

Vien noticed, and his eyes filled with concern. "You're serious about this."

"What were you dreaming about before Melinda's screaming woke you?" Plum asked.

"The school was filled with dragonflies," Vien said. "Nothing too strange." The divot between his eyebrows deepened. "Gwendle was with me, but we couldn't find Artem, or you."

"I haven't been able to sleep at all," Plum said, "and I would be willing to bet Artem hasn't, either."

"We need to find Gwendle and Artem and

figure this out," Vien said. "Our dreams have never meant anything before, but this time you were awake when Melinda tried to warn you about this."

He didn't suggest bringing this to the attention of their professors, or Dr. Abarrane, and Plum was grateful for that. It meant he shared the same inexplicable, nagging sense that this was meant to be a secret.

They didn't have to go far to find Gwendle. She was already on her way back to the bedroom. But Artem wasn't in the thinning crowd. He wasn't in his bed, either.

And after a thorough search of the dormitory, it seemed he wasn't anywhere to be found at all.

CHAPTER 5

It was eight o'clock in the morning exactly. Plum sat on the leather couch outside Dr. Abarrane's office, tallying up how many hours it had been since she'd slept. It had been nearly two o'clock in the morning when she woke up from the dream about Artem in the tall grasses, and she hadn't slept a blink since then. It was a very unusual sensation.

"Thirty hours," she muttered to herself. "That can't be right."

Vien and Gwendle sat at either side of her.

The three of them were holding hands, something they often did without realizing it. Dreams weren't the only thing they shared. Despite their vastly different personalities and interests, they often seemed to have the same thoughts.

Right now they were all thinking about Artem, who hadn't turned up since the incident with Melinda screaming at the piano.

Plum in particular was thinking about the thunder that growled and erupted outside, and the rain that sounded like an unsteady round of bewildered applause.

They had been waiting for more than twenty minutes to speak to Dr. Abarrane. Plum could feel each second blurring by. Seconds that were being wasted. She was frequently frustrated with Brassmere's rules about order and calm, but today it felt especially dire. Every second wasted here was a second that should be spent looking for Artem.

He couldn't have gone far, Plum reasoned. There would be no way through the gate without a key. And nobody else would have found their way inside to hurt him, because the gargoyles had been known to eat anyone who might try.

But he could be hurt. Or frightened.

The next clap of thunder made Gwendle flinch. She looked as though she might cry.

Vien was composed, but that didn't mean he was calm. He kept looking at Plum, no doubt fretting about the increasingly dark circles under her eyes. Plum knew how awful she looked— she'd caught a glimpse of herself in the mirror and cringed. But there had been more important things to contend with.

She was the first to speak, in a whisper so low that Gwendle and Vien had to lean close to her to hear. "What will we tell him?"

"The truth," Vien said. He had been giving this a lot of thought, Plum could tell.

Gwendle shook her head. "No. I can't explain it, but I have a sense that we shouldn't."

Gwendle was always very intuitive. Perhaps even a bit psychic, Plum had often thought.

They couldn't come to an agreement on what to tell Dr. Abarrane, but it turned out not to matter, because when the door opened and Dr. Abarrane invited the three of them into his office, he didn't ask for an explanation. Instead, as the three students sat in the chairs on the other side of his desk, he looked at Plum.

"How long has it been since you've slept, Plum?" he asked. He was not a large man. He was short and round, with a thick head of hair so gray that it was almost blue. But his voice was very big, Plum thought. The voice of a giant. The voice of a warrior going off to battle. Sometimes he took the form of these things in her dreams. Several students at Brassmere appeared in their tandem dreams, always in some new form, such as a spider or a kangaroo. Once there had even been a pink lake that had somehow resembled a girl with pigtails and freckles who nearly outran Plum on the track.

"Thirty hours and twenty minutes, sir," Plum answered.

Behind the lenses of his round glasses, Dr. Abarrane looked at the children's linked hands.

"We need to do something about that," he said. "If you can't sleep, you can't dream. And if you can't dream—well, no good can come of that, now, can it?"

Plum did not understand the significance of her dreams. None of the students at Brassmere knew why they were exceptional, or what it mattered. But Plum knew that without her dreams, her mind was starting to feel hazy and wrong. Colors seemed dull. Her head felt heavy.

She could feel Vien and Gwendle watching her, fretting quietly. Dr. Abarrane nodded to each of them. "I trust the two of you can find your own way to your classes this morning."

Vien blinked, confused. "Sir?"

Dr. Abarrane smiled, all the creases on his face appearing like lines freshly drawn. "Leave Plum to me. It's all right. Off with you now."

Plum nodded at each of them. She was so

tired. The second hand in the clock on the wall felt like a pounding hammer. "I'll be okay," she told them, and she knew that this wasn't a lie. No matter what happened to any of them, things always turned out for the best. They were all safe here.

She felt Vien's hesitation in particular when he and Gwendle left the room. But then the door closed behind them, and she heard their footsteps getting farther away down the polished hallway.

A slight smile appeared on Dr. Abarrane's face. "I remember the day I found you in particular, you know," he said. "You were the very first." Plum had heard this story before, of course, but she never grew tired of it. Sometimes, when she was by herself and feeling strangely lonely about things, she thought of it. If she thought hard enough, she could even see it playing out:

A rainy November night, ice cold. On an empty street with no houses for miles, a church had caught fire after an altar boy had neglected to blow out the candles before leaving for the evening. It was dark as ink and windy.

An infant had been left on the front steps, in a wooden crate from the farmers' market, the juice from its plums still staining the slats of it. The infant might have frozen to death if not for the warmth of the flames. And the flames might have burned her alive, except rather than swallowing the plum crate and the baby inside it, the flames formed a protective ring around her.

This was how Dr. Abarrane found her, and how he knew that she was something exceptional.

Plum was the first child Dr. Abarrane found, but she was soon to be joined by more than a dozen others. Some were found in orphanages, and others were the lone survivors of horrific accidents. Vien was found in the wreckage of a shredded Cadillac, and Gwendle was buried in the rubble of a cottage that had been half swallowed by a sinkhole.

Artem had been left right at the gate, under the protective watch of the stone gargoyles, wrapped in a red plaid ascot like a baby bird in a nest.

Dr. Abarrane's smile faded. "Plum, I don't know where Artem is, but I need you to find him."

"You'd like me to go out and search?" she asked.

He opened the drawer of his desk. "No." He extracted a key, long and slender and rusted. "Follow me."

Plum followed him down the hall and into the infirmary. It was a large wing with several curtained-off beds and a nursery, which would be filled with new arrivals soon, Plum suspected. Brassmere was never without babies for long. They always seemed to find their way to where they belonged.

Nurse Penny stood from her desk when she saw them arrive. She opened her mouth to speak, but stopped when she saw the key in Dr. Abarrane's hand.

"Plum is going to need a quiet place to rest," he said.

Whatever this meant, Nurse Penny seemed to understand. The key she turned opened a door that Plum had always assumed was a medicine closet, in no small part due to the sign above the knob that read Supplies.

But once the door had been opened, Plum realized it was not a closet at all, but a short hallway that led to four other locked doors, one of which responded to the same key. That door led to a small study, with floor-to-ceiling books and a green leather divan with an oversize matching pillow. There was a window, but upon further inspection, Plum realized that it was fake, its scenery of a sunlit valley painted in oils.

It was the window that frightened Plum. Suddenly, she felt very far from Brassmere. Far from Vien and Gwendle, and especially Artem. But she did not let her fear show. She had never been a skittish one, and she didn't want Dr. Abarrane or Nurse Penny to think she was weak.

"There's nothing to worry about," Nurse Penny said. She was very kind—the kindest person at Brassmere by far. "This is just another branch of the infirmary. Go ahead and lie down."

Tentatively, Plum lay on the divan. The leather was soft and warm. The pillow was filled with feathers.

"Just relax now," Dr. Abarrane said. "You're going to rest, and soon, you'll be as good as new."

CHAPTER 6

Though she knew this was a dream, Plum remembered that it was raining outside. She could still hear the dull patter of it hitting the roof. She could smell the oak from the fire, and the odd perfumed polish of the leather divan where she'd fallen asleep.

She looked up, and the clouds were speaking to one another. "Alert me of any changes to her vitals," Dr. Abarrane's voice was saying.

Nurse Penny was answering him, but her voice was farther away, and it echoed. ". . . experimental drug . . . could be dangerous . . ."

Plum didn't hear anything Dr. Abarrane said, except for one word: urgent.

Then they were both gone.

You're dreaming, Plum reminded herself. *Vien and Gwendle aren't here. They're in class. It's the daytime.*

Isn't it?

As she had this thought, the sky turned light and the clouds began to disperse. She was in the grand foyer at Brassmere, and the piano was playing itself.

"Melinda?" Plum asked. She knew that if she saw Melinda, it wouldn't really be her. Whenever she, Vien, Gwendle, or Artem saw someone they knew in their dream, they referred to them as a ghost. They weren't real, and anything they said was merely a projection of the friends' own thoughts.

But no one answered Plum, not even a ghost. One after another, the keys moved to the tune of the strange song Melinda had played the night before.

Plum moved for the hallway. All the bedroom doors were closed, and when Plum tried to open one of them, she realized that they were not doors at all. They were merely paintings.

The hallway went on and on forever, stretching into an unreachable darkness.

"Hello?" she called out, her voice strong and clear. There was an echo, like in the cave the last time she dreamed. She had a sense that she was supposed to be somewhere important.

But this dream felt strange; even in this state, she knew that something was wrong with her sleep. She was too aware of the room that Dr. Abarrane and Nurse Penny had led her to. She could feel the faint prick of the needle in her arm, though when she looked down at herself, nothing was there. She rubbed at the bright blue vein in the crease of her left arm, where she knew the IV needle was imbedded.

Thunder shook the walls. Plum spun around to face the giant windows that made up the grand foyer. The sky had turned deep gray with churning clouds and wild flashes of lightning. Though none of the windows were open, a breeze rolled through the room, making the piano keys flutter as though they were stacks of paper weighed down by a rock. Their music was faint and fluttery and erratic.

"Plum?" a voice called to her, so faint she nearly missed it. "Plum, where are you?"

"Artem?" She staggered left and right, trying to follow the sound. "Artem!"

"You have to leave Brassmere," Artem said. His voice was nearly lost over the wind. It had gotten much harsher, and Plum hugged her arms, shivering. Her dark hair whipped sharply to one side. "You have to get out."

Plum ran for the door and pulled at the heavy oak handle. It didn't budge. "How?" she asked. "How did you get out?"

Something growled, and when Plum looked out the window, through the gray and the flying leaves, she saw the dark, lumbering shadow of a monster. It was tall and hunched, almost like a bear but with long, sharp ears. It looked at her, its eyes flashed red.

Plum was not one to shy away from monsters in dreams, but she had the sense that somehow this monster was different. There was no sense in hiding. The hallway and all the doors behind her were painted. There was nowhere to go but forward.

She tried the handle again, and this time, the door swung open.

The air outside turned white, the wind and rain violent. She could barely see through the gloom of it as she moved forward. "Artem!" She kept calling his name.

The monster growled in the trees, and Plum followed the sound. If this monster was so determined to have her attention, then fine. There was probably a reason for it.

"What do you want?" she called out. She

stood still, her hair and clothes soaked. The monster emerged before her. Its fur was matted and gray, filled with bits of twigs and caterpillars and various forest things.

It was a great, lumbering thing, with tiny dark eyes and an enormous mouth filled with yellow fangs.

It seemed perplexed that Plum wasn't afraid, and it canted its head curiously at her, giving another fearsome growl.

Plum was not easy to scare, as this thing was bound to learn. But she was curious where this monster had come from. It didn't seem like the sort of thing she would create. It was more Artem's doing. Poor Artem, who was always so frightened of what things might be lurking in the shadows of his dreams, was the cause of so many monsters they spent their nights battling.

"What have you done with Artem?" she asked the monster, as though she were merely asking directions to the tea shop.

The monster opened its mouth again, and this time it didn't growl. This time, its mouth became so wide that it was big enough to devour a girl like Plum in a single bite. And that's what it did. The monster grabbed Plum in its clawed paws and, before she could do a thing to stop it, ate her.

CHAPTER 7

Being eaten by a monster would normally be the sort of thing that woke Plum from her sleep.

But as she fell through the bottomless damp darkness of the monster's throat, she felt her arm still throbbing. In the waking world, the needle was still in her arm, she knew. She remembered the strange purple liquid that had trailed from the bag and down the tube into her skin. Something within her began to panic, and she battled it down, a monster of its own.

It's only a dream, she reminded herself, as she

fell and fell for what seemed like years. *This has to end sometime.* If Vien, Gwendle, or Artem were here, this dark tunnel of monster mouth would not have lasted this long. One of them would have dreamed up an end to it.

But Plum was alone. Artem had stopped calling to her. She tried to shout for him, but found that she had no voice when she opened her mouth.

For the first time, in this dream, Plum began to panic. She'd always felt safe in even her most dangerous of dreams because she knew that she would wake up if she died. But she was not allowed to wake up this time. Maybe she had died. Maybe the monster swallowing her whole was enough to kill her in this dream, and now she would be trapped here until the needle was extracted from her arm.

Dr. Abarrane had seemed so worried about her, and she had been so tired, so desperate for sleep that she hadn't questioned the purple liquid in the IV bag. It was not uncommon practice for students at Brassmere to receive similar treatments for various things—insomnia, broken bones, inconsolable anxieties. Dr. Abarrane's treatments always helped. They always did.

But Plum needed to wake up now, and she couldn't.

Then, her feet touched the ground. Anxiety surged through her, a mix of wonder and relief that her fall had at last come to an end.

She was on a cobblestoned street now, in a city that didn't resemble Brassmere's campus at all. There was a tall clock tower just ahead, its bold yellow face glowing against the fog. The numbers on the clock face were replaced with odd symbols, and the hands moved in erratic patterns. This was common in dreams, where time made no sense.

The city itself gurgled and groaned, and Plum remembered that she was in the belly of the monster that had eaten her. Bits of bloody fur stuck to the brick faces of the surrounding buildings. It was damp here. Rain drizzled into puddles. And the sky had no stars.

All the windows in all the buildings were dark, except for one. She followed the cobblestone pathway to the only illuminated window in the city.

The window was large, almost the size of the building itself. As Plum drew nearer, it became obvious that the three people on the other side of the window couldn't see her. Interesting. They must have been ghosts, Plum thought, or figments of her imagination.

The window revealed one room, which appeared to be a sort of office, with a steel desk and stacks of papers raining down from shelves along the walls. At one side of the desk sat a man, in a peculiar uniform Plum had never seen before. It was all blue, with a gold star pinned to the breast pocket. Even without being close enough to read the word, Plum knew what it said: Sheriff.

Sheriff. This was a word she didn't know in the waking world. She was certain she'd never heard it anywhere before.

On the other side of the desk sat a woman and a man. Their chairs were pushed together, and they were holding each other's hands. They were crying.

They were beautiful, Plum thought. The woman had short dark hair, upon which was pinned a small hat bejeweled with stones and amber-colored feathers. She wore a long, simple brown dress. Her lips were painted peach pink, and her eyes were dark and glistening with tears.

The man wore a pinstriped suit with a handkerchief tucked neatly into its pocket, folded in a perfect triangle.

They were very much in love with each other, this man and woman. Somehow Plum knew this.

The woman blew her nose into a cloth handkerchief with lace trim. Plum could see all the fine details in the lace even from where she stood. That was the fascinating thing about dreams: little pieces of the world Plum never noticed when she was awake suddenly became beautiful.

The man with the gold star folded his hands and hunched forward on his desk. "We're going to do everything we can to find her," he said.

This only made the woman sob louder. The sound of those sobs echoed in all the dark alleyways and between the stars themselves.

The light in the window began to dim. The man and the woman started to fade. "Wait!" Plum cried. "Don't go."

They had never really been there, Plum knew. They were just ghosts. But something in her chest ached for them.

It was no matter. They didn't hear her. She pressed her hands to the glass just as it all disappeared.

Plum looked around to discover that she was alone again in a strange city that seemed to be empty.

"You were right." Artem's voice. A moment later, he materialized from the blackness of an alleyway. He was lit up by the glow of the clock tower.

"Artem!" Plum ran to him and threw her arms around him. "There you are! Where have you been?" This was not a ghost. Plum knew the difference. He was asleep and dreaming and had found his way to her here.

When he hugged her back, his arms felt weak. Plum drew back and held him by the shoulders as she inspected him. His cheeks were gaunt, his eyes ringed with dark lines, much worse than they'd been the last time she saw him. And all her elation at finding him turned into a deep and heavy dread that sat in her stomach.

"You were right to keep our dream from Dr. Abarrane." He grabbed her wrists. "Plum, listen to me, you can't tell them anything. You have to lie to them. Say you dreamed about the usual things, but don't tell them what you just saw."

Plum shook her head. "I don't understand. What did I just dream? Who were those people?"

"I don't know," Artem said. "But I've been having dreams like this for a while. People who are searching and searching for something they can't ever find."

"But that's impossible," Plum said. "I'm there for all your dreams, and I've never seen them."

Artem looked so sad. His mouth turned pensively downward, and he had trouble looking into her eyes. This wasn't like him at all, and it worried her and filled her with sympathy. She wanted desperately to console him. "I haven't told you everything," he said. "I thought it was a fluke, at first. I'd have dreams where I was in this city. I saw two people looking for something. Something important, but I could never figure out what it was. They didn't see me. It never lasted for very long. Soon enough it would all fade and I'd meet up with you and Vien and Gwendle."

"Why didn't you tell us?" Plum asked. She tugged at one of his brown curls affectionately, trying to reassure him. It didn't work; he didn't offer so much as a fleeting smile. "We would have helped you figure out what was going on."

"I was scared." Artem's eyes were wide. "I thought something was wrong with me. I thought—I thought—well, just that something was wrong, that's all. I didn't tell anybody, but the pinks knew something was amiss when they monitored my pulse. They told Dr. Abarrane I was hiding something and that I was no longer to be trusted. I don't know, maybe Dr. Abarrane has never trusted me, Plum."

"What did Dr. Abarrane say?"

Artem's grip on her wrists tightened. "Plum, listen to me. When you wake up, you can't tell him that you saw me here. You have to warn Vien and Gwendle. He's going to come for them, too. He's going to come for you."

"I don't understand." Plum's voice was breathless. "Who is coming for us? Why? Where are you?"

"Promise me," was all Artem said.

And then the dream disappeared.

CHAPTER 8

Plum awoke, feeling groggy and strange. The persistent aching in her left arm followed her back into the waking world, and her eyes shifted to the IV that was being extracted now by Nurse Penny's gentle hands.

"That was quite a long sleep," Nurse Penny said. "I understand you needed it. How are you feeling now?"

Plum was grateful that the pinks weren't here to monitor her pulse, because she was sure that it would betray her lie. Her heart had been betraying her a lot lately. "Much better," she said.

Smiling, Nurse Penny opened the drawer of the nightstand beside the divan where Plum lay. She extracted a yellow notepad and a black pen. "Here," she said. "It's not quite as pretty as your dream journal, but it will do in a pinch."

Plum sat up. Her head felt light, but she didn't let on. Rather, she smiled and took the notepad and said, "Thank you."

Nurse Penny patted her cheek. "I'll let Dr. Abarrane know that you're awake. Take a little time to reorient yourself."

Nurse Penny left the room, and the moment she closed the door behind her, Plum squeezed her eyes shut. A wave of fear rose up in her, so heavy and fast that it stole her breath. Her breaths came in quick bursts.

Stay calm, she told herself. She thought of the mountain made of rocks in the training center, and the first time she climbed it without wires. She hadn't let herself be frightened because she had convinced herself that falling was not an option. *Climb*—she had told herself—*or die.*

This was like that. She just had to keep going until she found Artem. He was okay. He had to be, because she would not accept that anything bad had happened to him. At the very least, she knew that he was alive—wherever he was—and that he had given her a warning.

Once she had steadied herself, she began to write. She had never been especially good at fiction—she'd been taught to always write the truth—but as it happened, she felt quite satisfied with her ability to spin a convincing lie. A girl who dreamed of such wild things night after night was bound to store some of it away should the need for a tale arise.

She wrote a dream of fanged antelope with dragon wings trying to tear her apart. She wrote about the crystal sword at her hip, how she had slain all of them and then spent the remainder of her dream luxuriating in a meadow of gold flowers that smelled of Nurse Penny's perfume, listening to the gentle babble of a nearby meadow. She wrote that it was just the rest she had needed.

An hour later, she sat in Dr. Abarrane's office as he read her notes. She studied his face, looking for any sign that he knew the dream was a lie. But he only chuckled as he read, and raised his brows, and occasionally looked pensive. When he was done reading, he said, "It sounds like you had a restful sleep."

"Yes," Plum said.

Dr. Abarrane set the pad on the table and folded his hands. "Plum," he said. "I like to think of all the students at Brassmere as my children, you know that. But your class—your generation—is especially dear to my heart. You're the ones who have made this school successful."

His face was so kind, Plum thought. She had always trusted him. Had always considered him a mentor, and the closest thing she had to a parent. But now when she looked at Dr. Abarrane, all she saw was Artem's pale and worried face, begging her not to trust this man she had trusted all her life.

Well, not *all* her life. There had been a few days in which Plum did not know Dr. Abarrane. A few days in which she had a mother and a father, or so she assumed. She was not born at Brassmere. No one was born at Brassmere. No one came here by choice.

He's going to come for you.

"You're here because you're exceptional, and Brassmere is the only place in the world that can challenge you," Dr. Abarrane went on. "You understand."

It wasn't a question, but Plum knew well enough to nod and say, "Yes. Of course."

"And it's imperative that you—that all of you—exercise complete honesty when you report those talents to us."

Plum sat with her back straight. She kept

track of her breathing, the way she always did with the pinks. She thought of Artem all alone with the pinks on their last report day, frightened and hiding such a big secret, and she wished she had known so she could have helped him. Plum was good at being composed. She was good at lying— not that she ever had a reason to. It was all in the body language. Plum found that if she appeared confident in what she was saying, it was rarely brought to question.

She could see, also, that Dr. Abarrane was not going to be so easy to fool. He opened a drawer of his desk, and then he placed a book on the table before Plum. Her dream journal.

She felt a chill in her blood at that, and even before he spoke, she knew what he was going to say.

He opened the journal, to the spot where Plum had torn away the other night's page.

Stay calm. It was Plum's mantra today. She weighed her options. She could deny that she had torn a page from the journal, but that would be easy to disprove. Despite her best efforts when she had torn it away, she could now see a tiny ribbon of shredded paper indicating her handiwork.

She could tell Dr. Abarrane the truth about the disturbing dream she'd had, but that would go against Artem's warning.

Or, she could lie.

She didn't have to work hard to give Dr. Abarrane a look of worry. "I had a nightmare the other night," she said. "That's why I've been unable to sleep ever since."

"Is that so?" Dr. Abarrane closed the journal. His voice was patient, but Plum no longer trusted him. In the span of a single dream on a single rainy morning, everything had changed. "Why don't you tell me about it?"

"I had a dream that Brassmere burned to the ground," Plum said. "Everyone was trapped inside, including me. We all died." She did her best to appear saddened. "I never told my friends about it. I didn't tell anyone. I thought— Well. I thought it would be bad luck to talk about it. Dragons and monsters are one thing, but a fire could really happen. It's the first time I dreamed about something that felt real."

Dr. Abarrane's expression softened, and Plum realized that he believed her. She wished that she could be excited about this, but all she could think about was Artem, trapped somewhere in the churning realms of dreams, and of Vien and Gwendle, who were probably wondering at this very moment what to do with their incomplete foursome.

"Have your dreams been especially strange lately?" Dr. Abarrane asked.

"My dreams are always strange," Plum answered.

"Yes, well, I do need you to write everything down." He tapped the journal pointedly. "There is a reason we monitor your abilities. We need to be sure that all is well."

"I'm sorry, sir," Plum said, and knew that this was another lie. She wasn't sorry, and she was through divulging anything about her abilities to Dr. Abarrane or anyone at Brassmere. She no longer knew who she could trust, except for her three best friends, one of whom was missing.

Dr. Abarrane glanced at the clock above the door. "You were asleep for several hours," he said. "I'd like you to rest some more. Nurse Penny will escort you to your dormitory." He smiled. "Get some rest, Plum. There's nothing to worry about."

"What about Artem?" Plum said. Her voice was calm, but she wanted to shout at him. She wanted to ask what he knew, what he had done. "Has anyone found him?"

Dr. Abarrane swiveled in his leather desk chair and glanced at the window behind him, with nothing to be seen but their own reflections in the glass. The wind and rain were embattled outside.

"There's a search party out looking for him," he said. "He will turn up. He can't have gotten far. Even if he'd wanted to, there's no way over the fence."

That was exactly what Plum was afraid of.

When Gwendle returned to the dormitory after dinner and found Plum sitting up in bed, she burst into tears and hugged her.

It was rare of Gwendle to cry. She used to do it all the time when they were small, so much so that the professors would punish her for it. After enough hours holding up pails of water outside the classroom door until her arms wobbled and ached, Gwendle learned to be very selective with whom she displayed her emotions.

Plum was so glad to see her that she almost could have cried, too. She wrapped her arms around her.

"I was so worried." Gwendle finally drew back, rubbing tears from her cheeks. "First Artem and then nobody would tell us where you'd gone.

Vien wanted to pound down Dr. Abarrane's door, and I had to plead for him not to."

"He wanted to do that for me?" Plum's voice came out soft and startled. A strange warmth stirred in her stomach at the thought of Vien willing to fight for her. But she forced the thought away. It wasn't practical, not when they had something much bigger to contend with. "Listen," Plum whispered, and Gwendle leaned in, her blue eyes wide. "I have something important to tell you and Vien, but not here."

Gwendle sat up straight and nodded, understanding. Plum didn't have to explain. There was only one place in which their secrets would be safe, and that was in their dreams.

CHAPTER 9

The dream began with the sound of wind. At first, Plum would have believed she was still awake, if not for the fact that she had wings. She was sitting in the grand foyer, on a gigantic tufted leather chair. It was bright pink—another sign that this was a dream.

Gwendle was the first to join her. She had been eager to get to sleep that night, even turning out the lights an hour early. She floated down from the chandelier, using it like a brass parachute held above her head. She landed soundlessly.

"Why are we at Brassmere?" she asked.

Plum looked around the room. "I don't think it's real," she said. "All the doors in that hallway are painted on."

"You're right." Gwendle's voice trailed as she considered this. "That's new."

Vien arrived next. He managed to use the front door, but struggled with the wind and rain as he tried to close it. "There's something out there," he said. "I didn't get a good look, but I heard it growling, and through the smog I thought I saw horns."

"I wanted to talk to you about that," Plum said.

Because this was a dream, the events of the day were further from all their minds. It was a constant struggle to remember what was real and what truly mattered.

"There you are," Vien said. The pink chair was gone, and Plum was standing now. Vien took her hands and held them tightly. "Where were you all evening? Dr. Abarrane said—"

"We can't trust him." Plum spoke hastily,

because she knew there was a monster outside and she knew that dreams were fickle and ever changing, and what she had to tell them was important.

Gwendle stood beside her now, too. "Can you tell us what happened now?"

"He gave me medicine that forced me to stay asleep," Plum said. "I couldn't wake up when I should have. I thought I had died in my dream, but instead it stayed black for a very long time, and then I saw something."

"What did you see?" Vien asked. He looked very worried, and Plum thought about what Gwendle had said about Vien wanting to pound down Dr. Abarrane's door.

"I was in a strange city," Plum said. "There were people, but they couldn't see or hear me. And then Artem was there."

"Was Artem a ghost or was he dreaming, too?" Vien's voice took on a new urgency. "Did he say where he is?"

"He was dreaming, too," Plum said. "It was really him. I'm positive. He was trying to warn us. He said that he'd had the same dream of that strange city, and he tried to keep it a secret, but Dr. Abarrane found out." The dream world fought with the waking world in Plum's mind. The dream tried to tell her to be calm, that nothing could hurt her here, that everything was all right. But everything was not all right, and Plum knew it. "I think Dr. Abarrane has done something with Artem. I think he's in danger. He told me that none of us are safe, but I woke up before he could explain."

"Are you sure it was really Artem?" Gwendle pressed. "Why would he say those things? Dr. Abarrane is our mentor. He—"

Before Gwendle could say another word, the doors to the grand foyer swung open with a burst of wind. It felt like a hurricane. Branches and bright autumn leaves and hunks of shrapnel filled the room.

"Hold on!" Plum clung to Vien's and Gwendle's hands. She sensed the monster before it appeared, gigantic and lumbering.

"Should we run?" Vien was shouting, his voice nearly lost to the wind.

"Won't matter," Plum said. "It's going to eat us, anyway."

"What?" Gwendle shrieked.

"Whatever you do, don't wake up," Plum yelled, and then the monster opened its great dark mouth and devoured them whole.

It was quieter once the monster had swallowed them; all the wind and the storm and the aggressive thunder gave way to the damp silence of a cave. They fell helplessly, but Plum managed to keep hold of Gwendle's and Vien's hands.

The fall was not as long this time, but the landing was harder. The three of them toppled to the ground with a series of grunts and groans.

"Is everyone okay?" Plum asked.

Gwendle sat up, a thin line of blood

streaming from her forehead and down her nose. Vien grunted and pushed himself up by his arms. Plum could see that he had injured his arm, but he was inspecting her for injuries rather than complain about it.

"I'm all right," Plum said, using her sleeve to dab at Gwendle's forehead.

"I'm okay, too," Gwendle said. "I think it's already healing itself. What is this place?"

They were on the same cobblestoned street that Plum had dreamed that evening. It was still nighttime, and Plum wondered if the sun ever rose here. The clock tower shone bright, its face full of nonsense numbers.

Vien's dark eyes were still on Plum. "You're dreaming us here." It wasn't a question. "What is this place?"

"This is where I saw Artem," she said.

Gwendle got to her feet and ran to the nearest alley. "Artem?" she said. "Are you here? Please come out. We're so worried."

A crash was the only answer, and then one of the houses burst into flames.

Gwendle jumped back, away from the blast of sudden heat. "Did this happen in your dream?" she asked.

"No." Plum rose to her feet, Vien at her side. "I didn't notice that house at all." She charged forward.

"What are you doing?" Vien ran to keep up with her.

"Whatever is in that fire, we're meant to see it, or else it wouldn't be here." Plum knew with certainty that she was not in control of this dream. She had no weapons. She had no sense of what would come next.

It was a small house, with a brick face and tiny windows on either side of a bright green door. The flowers in the window boxes were the first to be eaten by the flames. Plum watched them disintegrate to ash, and a strange sense of longing and grief threatened to overwhelm her.

Something about those flowers—something about this house—felt familiar.

Walking right through a wall of roiling flames, she kicked the door open and stepped inside.

Vien and Gwendle stumbled after her, all three of them coughing. Vien said something about dreaming up a mask to protect their mouths, but Plum couldn't hear him, and, anyway, no such masks appeared.

The house was lit bright by the flames, filled with black clouds of smoke. Plum saw the body clearly, as though a spotlight shone over that section of the floor.

"Wait," she said. Her voice was suddenly clear and loud. The flames and smoke carried on, but they had gone silent.

Blood rushed in Plum's ears.

She took one step closer to the body, then another, until she was close enough to make out all the details. It was the same woman she'd dreamed of that evening, in the same elegant clothes. Her dark hair spilled over one shoulder. Plum knelt before her and peeled the hair from the woman's face to have a better look. Her eyes were open and dark and dead.

"No," Plum whispered. "You can't be dead. You can't be."

She tried to shake the woman awake, tried to will the dream to bend to her wishes. But her efforts were in vain.

"Plum." Vien's voice was soft as he and Gwendle knelt at either side of her. "She isn't real. She's just a ghost."

"She's not a ghost," Plum cried, and she saw Vien's startled expression at that. She sounded as though she was about to cry. She never cried. "She's *real*. If she were a ghost, we could make her come back to life. This entire place is real. Look at it. When have any of us ever dreamed of anything like this?"

"She's right," Gwendle agreed sympathetically. She touched the woman's forehead. "This place is all wrong. There are no weapons. No escape routes. The flames are all silent, and none of us silenced them."

As if on cue, the roar of the flames returned. There was a crash as the staircase collapsed in on itself. And then they all heard it. The distinct, unmistakable sound of a baby crying.

"That wasn't coming from in here," Gwendle said. She nodded to a window on the far wall. The heat from the flames had shattered the glass. "It's outside."

There was no time for Plum to have a good look. The house collapsed in the ruin of the flames, and the dream came to an end.

Plum came awake first, gasping. Across the room, Gwendle popped upright in her bed several seconds later. She was coughing, as though she still believed she was surrounded by flames.

She met Plum's gaze. They wore the same worried and serious expression.

"What was that?" Gwendle whispered.

"I don't know," Plum whispered back. She

tried to look at it logically. Logic would help, while worry would not. "But Artem has been seeing it for a while, and when Dr. Abarrane found out about it, Artem disappeared."

Gwendle considered this, and her face turned sad. To know that Dr. Abarrane might do anything to harm them was a very big betrayal.

"Dr. Abarrane is checking our dream journals," Plum said. "He'll probably check them in the morning when we leave for class. We have to come up with a convincing lie."

That would be easy enough. They were all well accustomed to the routine oddities of their dreams.

Gwendle grabbed her journal and climbed onto Plum's bed. Together, they huddled over her flashlight and worked out the plot of a convincing dream. In it, there had been a cottage in the woods made entirely of snakes. They wielded weapons made of rubies, and as they fought off the snakes, Vien sustained a poisonous bite that turned his eyes neon green. They spent the rest of the dream trying to climb a mountain whose crest had the antidote.

They planned to visit Vien and tell him their plan, but a soft knock at their dormitory door told them they didn't have to.

Vien sat on the floor, huddled over his own journal, offering his own suggestions. Gwendle needed an animal to help them scale the mountain, so she'd managed to lure a giant salamander with gossamer scales to help them along the way.

Artem was not there.

Plum stared at the empty lines at the bottom half of her page.

"We'll find him," Vien reassured her, reading her mind, as he always seemed to do.

"We should talk to Melinda, too," Gwendle said. "She might know something, after what happened to her last night."

"Was she in class?" Plum asked.

"Not in the morning, but in the afternoon,"

Gwendle said. "She seemed—well, actually, she looked a little like you and Artem did when you weren't able to get back to sleep."

They're coming for us. Plum replayed those words in her head for what felt like the hundredth time. The words Melinda had said that night in her trance over the piano. The warning Artem gave in her dream.

CHAPTER 10

They all agreed that it was important to act normal. That was key. Dr. Abarrane would be watching them. And maybe the professors would as well. Acting normal did not mean pretending that everything was fine, as Vien had pointed out. Acting normal meant asking their professors about Artem, even though they knew they would not be given an answer. It meant being attentive in class, even though their minds were filled with images of the burning house and the woman's body and the baby crying through the broken window.

It meant staying calm. It meant questioning everything.

Their first chance to talk to Melinda came after lunch, during physical training.

It was a cold autumn day, and each gust of wind shook more bright and dying leaves from the bare, scrawny fingers of their branches.

The triplets were engaged in a sparring match, each of them wielding a slender silver sword. Blood was frequently drawn during these, and several of the younger students sat on the grass watching with morbid fascination. It wasn't the swordsmanship so much as the concept of siblings that intrigued them. The triplets all had matching black hair cut at various lengths, and matching dark eyes that all bore different expressions.

Melinda, like most students, was usually interested in watching these sparring matches. Today, though, she was scaling the rock wall. She moved quickly, fluidly, like a creature trying to claw its way up to the sun.

After brief deliberation, Plum, Vien, and Gwendle agreed that Plum should be the one to go up and talk to her, in no small part because Plum was an excellent climber with flawless equilibrium.

They agreed it would raise less suspicion if they didn't approach Melinda together. Dr. Abarrane wasn't here to oversee the training activities, but after Artem's warning, they no longer trusted any of their professors, or even the nurses who stood on the sidelines, prepared for any emergency.

All day they had done an impressive job of acting normal, and Plum was quite proud of herself for this.

Still, as Plum scaled the rocks, she wished Gwendle could come along with her. Gwendle was friendly, and good at putting people at ease. Plum was not. Professor Nayamor had a saying that Plum was "all business, no fluff."

The rock wall was a quarter-mile high, and

Melinda was already at the top. As Plum made her trek, she thought about how best to approach her. *What would Gwendle do?* Gwendle would ask questions, Plum thought, be interested, be friendly.

There were other students climbing the rock mountain, but they wouldn't make it to the top. Few ever did, especially now in the autumn when the wind was like a cold slap every time it blew.

There was a small ledge at the top of the mountain, and that's where Melinda sat when Plum reached her. Her legs were hugged to her chest, and her chin was rested on her knee. When Plum climbed up beside her, Melinda's eyes moved toward her but then returned to the horizon. From up here, they could see over the spiked iron gate that surrounded Brassmere. There was nothing but trees—rich, full, colorful trees whose leaves fell and fell but whose branches never went bare.

"Hi," Plum said, settling beside her.

Melinda's arms tightened around her knees.

Be interested, Plum reminded herself. *Be friendly. Ask questions.*

"How are you feeling?" Plum asked. Melinda looked awful, pale and drawn, her eyes glassy and ringed with dark lines. But she'd had the energy to climb this far, so she couldn't have been too ill, Plum thought, or she had just been that desperate to get away.

"I'm sorry," Melinda said. "About Artem. I hope that they find him soon."

Plum blinked, surprised. "Thank you."

"I know how close you are," Melinda went on. "That's nice, you know? That you get along so well with the classmates you share your abilities with. Trina, James, and Clayton are nice enough, but I don't think they like me much."

"It's because you're the best at what you do," Plum said. "People don't like you when you're the best at things." Plum knew a lot about that. There were many students at Brassmere who grumbled whenever she accomplished something in record time, or received praise from one of her professors.

Melinda smiled, but her eyes were still glassy and faraway. "Sometimes, I fail on purpose," she said. "I let Trina bend spoons, and I let James unwind the screws from the puzzles we're assigned to. I pretend that I'm too tired, or too weak, so that they won't think I'm stuck-up." She laughed a little at that. "It's stupid, I know."

"You shouldn't do that," Plum said. "You shouldn't hold yourself back just to make them like you."

"I know," Melinda said. "You're lucky is all; I've always been a bit jealous of you. Sharing abilities is one thing, but sharing dreams? That must be really special. I always feel so alone in my dreams. Especially when I wake up."

Though they were alone and no one could possibly hear them, Plum lowered her voice. "Have you dreamed about anything strange?" she asked.

"Is this about the other night, with the piano?" Melinda said. Her expression turned cautious. "I don't remember anything about that. I only remember waking up, bleeding."

Plum hesitated. Far below, Gwendle and Vien were poised side by side at the track. After a beat, they took off running, their shoes making hard splashes in the puddles from yesterday's rain.

"Do you remember what you said to me?" Plum asked.

Melinda shook her head. "I don't even remember you being there. That whole night is a blur." She winced. "Why? Did I say something terribly strange?"

Plum decided not to tell her the truth. Not yet. It was going to be a lot to take in, and though Melinda had always been friendly enough, Plum wasn't sure yet that she could trust her. All the students at Brassmere were loyal to Dr. Abarrane, and she couldn't risk Melinda telling him about this conversation.

The safest course to take was to ask questions,

Plum reminded herself. Let Melinda do the talking. That way, Melinda would have no reason to go to Dr. Abarrane at all. She wasn't going to tell on herself.

"What's it like to be alone in your dreams?" Plum asked.

"Normal, I suppose," Melinda said. "Nobody is real, so they all say and do whatever I imagine. It's like I'm directing a play, and I know I'm supposed to be in charge, but the actors all sort of run amok."

How strange, Plum thought. Normal dreams were filled with ghosts. Only the dreamer was real.

Vien was winning his race against Gwendle. He usually did. But it hardly mattered to them. Plum supposed she *was* lucky to be so closely bonded to them. Whatever tensions arose among other classmates, Vien, Gwendle, and Artem had always been her sanctuary.

"Have you had any dreams that felt especially strange?" Plum ventured, hopeful and cautious.

Immediately she knew that she had made a mistake. She could feel Melinda's unease.

"I should get back," Melinda said. "Professor Nayamor doesn't like us to spend too much time on one activity."

"Wait," Plum said, but Melinda was already climbing down.

Plum went after her, keeping pace. She wished Gwendle were here. Gwendle probably would have had her answers by now. But where Plum excelled at running and fencing and slaying imaginary demons in her dreams, she was terrible at making friends. Or talking to people at all, really.

"I wasn't going to tell anyone, if that's what you're worried about," Plum said, speaking hastily. She knew that once they reached the ground, her only chance to talk to Melinda would be over. "Please. I just want to find Artem."

"I can't help you." Melinda wouldn't look at her. She maneuvered the footholds expertly; she really was quite talented, Plum realized, for a girl who was so shy and modest.

Desperate, Plum grabbed her wrist. "Please," she said.

Melinda jerked her hand away, but she stopped climbing. "You can't do that." Hesitantly, she looked down to the nurse standing at the edge of the training arena, then back at Plum. "You're going to get us in trouble," she said. "They're watching. They're always watching." When she started descending again, she moved slower. "Like I said, I hope you find your friend. But I can't help you."

CHAPTER 11

At dinnertime, the cafeteria was quieter than usual. The students were all hunched around one another, speaking in whispers and hushed voices as they ate. Plum couldn't hear what was being said, but she knew they were talking about Artem. A student disappearing from Brassmere was unheard of. Nobody entered or left the campus except for the pinks, or sometimes Dr. Abarrane when he went to search for new orphans with exceptional abilities.

All day, students had been approaching Plum,

Vien, and Gwendle to offer their sympathies, which only thinly veiled their desire for gossip. They didn't care about Artem, not really. They didn't know who he really was, he was so shy and quiet. If he never came back, he would become a sort of ghost story for them to tell. A game.

It compounded Plum's misery. She had not stopped thinking about Artem since he'd disappeared, and while she considered herself an expert at solving puzzles and riddles and problems, now that it was important, she had nothing.

"It's my fault," Plum muttered. She stared at her dinner: buttery roasted potatoes and a leg of honey-glazed chicken, garnished by string beans. It was one of her favorite dishes, but she wasn't hungry. "I tried to get too much out of her. All I did was make her suspicious of me."

"It's not your fault," Vien said. "If she does know something, of course she's not just going to come out with it right away. You wouldn't, either, right?"

"No." Plum nudged the potatoes around with her fork, sulking. "But she knows something. I could see it on her face. She's scared, and she doesn't know who to trust."

"She'll come around," Gwendle said, and smiled reassuringly. "We'll figure something out."

That night, Plum lay awake for more than an hour after the lights had gone out, listening to the wind. She thought about Artem, alone wherever he was, out there in the cold.

Across the room, Gwendle had long since fallen asleep. She and Vien would be waiting for her, Plum knew. She closed her eyes for what must have been the hundredth time tonight, and vowed that this time she would not open them again until morning.

Eventually, the menacing wind became a fitful lullaby, and Plum dozed off.

When she opened her eyes within her dream,

at first, Plum was alone. She was standing in a hallway with white tiles and white walls, and the smell of something harsh that burned in her nostrils. The only window was on an inner wall, revealing another room within this building, rather than whatever was outside it.

Plum approached, and puzzled at what she saw. The window revealed a room with dim lighting, and two dozen plastic cradles holding two dozen babies who wriggled lazily in their blankets.

Plum marveled at that. She had seen babies at Brassmere, of course, but students weren't allowed to linger in the nursery.

But this wasn't Brassmere. Plum didn't know what this place was. It was so sterile and blank, entirely unlike anything she usually dreamed. It felt like being in a notebook with nothing written on its pages.

One of the babies cried out, piercing the calm silence.

A door opened on the far wall, and in walked a nurse whose face was very familiar. She hurried to the crying infant, plucking it from its cradle. "Shh, shh, it's all right," she was saying.

As soon as Plum heard her voice, she recognized her as Nurse Penny. She looked different in this dream. Her copper hair, normally long and braided, was cut to her chin, and her face was rounder. She looked only a few years older than Plum. Still a teenager, even.

Nurse Penny glanced at the window briefly, but she didn't see Plum standing at the other side of it. Just like in the dreams of the cobblestoned city, this place was also outside Plum's control, the ghost of Nurse Penny like a marionette that had broken free of its strings and developed its own mind.

The baby was soothed by Nurse Penny's efforts. "You know it's time for your special treat, don't you?" Nurse Penny said. "Always the intuitive one."

She carried the baby from the room, and the window faded away, leaving only a wall in its place.

Odd, Plum thought. She tried to will the window back into existence, but nothing happened.

She heard footsteps approaching in haste from one end of the hall. Dr. Abarrane and two of the Brassmere nurses were running alongside a gurney. They didn't see Plum, and she stepped back to avoid being stampeded.

In a split-second decision, Plum jumped onto the end of the gurney as it raced onward. There was a child lying atop it, red and gasping with fever, gleaming with sweat. An IV bag was trailed into his arm.

"I want a full list of every drug administered this morning," Dr. Abarrane was demanding. Like Nurse Penny, he was also much younger here. "This child was perfectly healthy when I saw him yesterday. He'd been able to lift the curio over his head."

So this child had an ability. He must have belonged to Brassmere, then.

Taking advantage of her invisibility, Plum leaned over the child to have a better look. She didn't recognize him. He was very young—five, maybe six—but Plum believed now that this dream was taking place in the past. If Nurse Penny and Dr. Abarrane were younger here than in the waking world, this child was likely older than Plum was now.

They burst through a set of swinging doors at the end of the hall.

The child was hastily connected to wires that led to a series of waiting machines.

Plum hopped off of the gurney and stood at a distance to watch.

"We gave him three doses of blue," one of the nurses was reading off of a chart. "The immediate effects were an increase in physical strength and energy. The fever began seven to eight hours after injection."

"Who else has received this dosage?" Dr.

Abarrane was standing over the child now, stroking his forehead in a gesture that Plum mistook for affection until she saw Dr. Abarrane peel open the boy's eyelid to check his pupils.

"No one, Doctor. He was our prototype."

A loud, flat beep filled the room. The sound was endless and excruciating, and it drowned out all else. The nurses and Dr. Abarrane continued to fret and fuss over the wires and the machines and the fluid in the IV.

But it was no use. The boy was dead.

CHAPTER 12

The beeping carried over into the next phase of Plum's dream, but it quickly faded as the scenery began to emerge.

Now she was lying on her back in a meadow, bright green and dotted with yellow flowers, under a clear blue sky.

Vien was sitting beside her. "Are you awake now?"

Plum pushed herself upright. "No," she said. "We're dreaming, aren't we?"

He laughed at that. Plum realized that it had

been days since she'd heard Vien laugh, but that it had felt like years. Everything in the waking world had become so dark and brutal and serious. She missed being happy. She missed not worrying so much.

"You've been sleeping in our dreams," Vien said. "That's a first."

"Where's Gwendle?" Plum asked.

Vien nodded skyward. A shadow flew across the sun. It was a great winged creature of some sort, Gwendle riding its back and shrieking with delight.

"We met each other here after we'd both fallen asleep, and we found you lying in the grass," Vien explained. "We couldn't wake you. So, Gwendle flew off to search for Artem and I stayed here in case you came back around." He looked at her. "Where were you? Do you remember?"

"I remember everything," Plum said. She waved to Gwendle, who eventually noticed and sailed back down to earth.

Plum told them about all she'd seen: the strange and sterile building, the nursery, and the boy she'd watched die on a gurney while Dr. Abarrane looked on.

"I know that this makes no sense," Plum said, "but I think what I saw was real. I think it happened in the past, and somehow I was able to see it."

"Is that possible?" Gwendle plucked a tiny dragon insect from her hair. It sailed dizzily skyward on gossamer wings. "Nothing that happens in our dreams has ever been real before."

"This felt real," Plum said. "It felt like Artem—" She cut herself off. She didn't want to say anything out loud until she was sure she'd sorted it out in her head. When she spoke again, she chose her words carefully, for this was a very strange situation. "I think Artem knows something, and that's why he disappeared. I think he's trying to warn us."

"Why doesn't he come out and tell us himself?" Vien asked.

"Maybe he can't," Plum said.

"He's only spoken to you," Vien went on, thinking aloud. "Maybe he's reaching out to all of us, but you're the only one strong enough to get the message."

Gwendle nodded in agreement, her eyes wide. "He's right. You're the only one who's been able to speak to Artem since he disappeared."

"But we all saw that burning house," Plum said.

"*You* dreamed us there," Vien said. "That monster who swallowed us was after you. It only took us along because you were holding on to us."

"If that's true," Plum said, "then we need to get Melinda to trust us. When she was in her trance, she said the same thing that he did. And the way she acted today on the mountain in the training arena—she definitely knows something, even if she doesn't know what it means."

The grass shifted and sighed, and Plum

realized it was not grass at all, but rather the grasslike scales of some gigantic creature Gwendle had dreamed.

Overhead, the sky filled with birds. Dozens of them, in a rainbow of colors.

"Look." Plum shielded her eyes and tilted her head skyward. Birds were Artem's trademark. "He's nearby. He's dreaming."

The three of them jumped to their feet. The birds began flying south, some of them straggling, flying in flourishing swirls and loops to amuse themselves. Definitely Artem's birds.

As they ran to keep up with the birds, the grasslike creature growled and stirred. It was pulling them in one direction while the birds went another. Plum ran faster and faster, and when she realized she was making progress despite the creature's efforts, she laughed in triumph.

She looked over her shoulder, and then she realized that Vien and Gwendle had fallen so far behind that she could no longer see them.

Above her, the sky turned gray and then rapidly black. Flashes of hot white lightning traced the outlines of churning clouds.

A voice was echoing through the sudden winds, calling her name.

"Artem?" She ran forward and then back, trying to follow the voice as it echoed all around her.

"Plum!" Artem cried. "You have to get out. They're coming for you. They're coming for all of us."

"What do you mean?" Her voice was desperate. She was so tired. So tired of being afraid and sad and worried. So tired of dreams that made no sense. So tired of not understanding what was happening, or knowing whom to trust. "Artem!"

This was still a dream. She knew it. But it felt very real. Her grief felt real, and she didn't even know what it was that she was grieving.

The giant animal below her feet twisted and bucked, and she was thrown into darkness.

A hand grabbed her wrist before she could

fall, yanking her so hard that her arm felt as though it might break.

"Hold on!" It was Artem. She looked up and saw him, on the edge of the creature's back, keeping her from dropping down into that endless darkness. "Try to give me your other hand."

She could barely hear him over the howling wind. Though she knew that this was a dream, Plum felt a very real sense of dread over what would happen to her if she slipped out of Artem's grasp. She remembered falling down the monster's throat when it had swallowed her, and thinking that she would be trapped in that bottomless nothing forever.

Plum focused on her core strength, remembering everything she'd been taught in the training arena. She managed to get one foot on the side of the monster, then the other. Then, with the last of her strength she raised her other arm to Artem's outstretched fingers.

His arms were shaking from the strain— another sign that this was no ordinary dream. In an ordinary dream, both of them would possess strength beyond what they could accomplish when they were awake.

But he didn't let go. He gritted his teeth and pulled, and Plum worked her feet against the side of the monster, giving herself leverage.

As she got closer to the surface, she clawed at the ground, and Artem grabbed her by the back of the collar, pulling her the rest of the way.

She landed on the ground beside him, and they both lay there for a few seconds, side by side, breathing hard as the adrenaline surged and then began to die down.

"Are you okay?" he asked.

"What is this place?" Plum said. "Why can't we control anything?"

"I don't know," Artem said. "I've been calling for all of you, and I can never find you. I walk around and walk around, and can never wake up or find a way out. I think I've been stuck here for years."

"You've been gone for days." Plum turned onto her side so that she was facing him. She studied his face, his tired eyes, his brown curls, his gaunt cheeks. He was not a ghost, she knew. "Have you been asleep this whole time?"

"I think so," Artem said. "Every time it seems like I might have woken up, something strange happens, and I realize I'm still dreaming."

"What's the last thing you remember?" Plum sat up.

He looked like he might cry. "I don't know. It's all foggy."

Plum knew that there was a lot for them to figure out, but all she saw in that moment was Artem. Sweet, ever-nervous Artem, who had been alone in this place for far too long.

"I've missed you," Plum said, pulling him into a hug. Artem clung to her, and she petted his hair. "I'll get you out," she said. "I promise. I won't leave you here alone."

Artem was the first to let go. He held her

shoulders. "You can't stay here forever," he said. "If there's one thing I've learned about this place, it's that the only way out must be in the waking world somewhere. You have to go back. Find where I'm sleeping and wake me up."

"You can't be outside," Plum reasoned. "You'd have frozen to death by now. But if you're at Brassmere, where could you be?"

"I remember going to sleep in my own bed," Artem said. "But that's it. Nothing weird."

Plum thought back to the morning Artem disappeared, when Dr. Abarrane and Nurse Penny brought her to that strange room and hooked an IV to her arm. She thought about falling down the monster's throat, when she knew it was time to wake up but her body wouldn't let her. How the dream of the cobblestoned city and the couple crying in the window only came to her because she'd been forced to stay asleep and dreaming.

"I think I know what's happening." She stood,

and Artem followed after her, confused. "You're being kept asleep by Dr. Abarrane. There's something he wants with your dreams. All those strange things you've been seeing—he must want you to learn something."

"But where?" Artem asked.

"I saw a place, in my dream," Plum said. "With all white walls and a funny smell to it. There were nurses giving medicine to a boy there." Plum didn't burden Artem with the knowledge that the boy in her dream had died. "I bet you're there."

Artem wrinkled his nose, as though he could suddenly smell it, too. "That doesn't sound like Brassmere."

"No," Plum agreed.

"But if it's not at Brassmere . . ." Artem hesitated. "Where is it?"

CHAPTER 13

Plum awoke without any warning. She opened her eyes and found herself back in her dormitory.

It was still dark out. The clock on the wall said it was after three in the morning.

She took a moment to collect her thoughts. Artem had just been with her, sharing their dream, and now, with Gwendle breathing evenly across the room, Plum felt terribly alone.

She was afraid, she realized. It was such an unusual thing that it took her a moment to admit that's how she felt. She was afraid, but she also knew what she had to do.

Quietly, she got out of bed and made her way to the closet. Gwendle didn't stir, even as the door creaked noisily on its hinges. Plum didn't know what Gwendle was dreaming, but she hoped it was something nice. She hoped that Gwendle and Vien weren't too worried about her.

She retrieved her wool coat from its hanger and buttoned it all the way to the chin. Then she opened the window and climbed outside. A cold breeze blew into the room. Gwendle shivered in her sleep and pulled the blanket tighter around herself.

Plum stayed still, frozen with one leg out the window, not daring to move until she was sure Gwendle was still asleep. Plum knew that she had to do this alone. She was the only one who had dreamed of Artem, and of the strange building with the white walls. She was the only one meant to find him.

Brassmere's campus was an entirely different place at night. The street lamps flickered as the wind blew. All the windows were dark and sleeping. The quiet was eerie. Even so, Plum kept thinking that she heard voices in the darkness, footsteps coming after her.

If Dr. Abarrane found her out here, what would he do? Force her into another sleep in which she dreamed and dreamed forever with no way out?

She shivered, and not from the cold. She moved faster, breaking into a run. She didn't stop until she had reached the iron gate. The bars were too narrow for her to squeeze through, so she began to climb. She braced one foot on either bar and shinnied her way to the top. It was very high, and the metal felt like ice even through her gloves.

Halfway up the gate, her adrenaline surged. Her heart pounded in her ears. It wasn't the treachery of the climb—she knew she could make it, and she had done far more rigorous climbs in the training arena. It was the realization that she was about to do what no student at Brassmere had ever accomplished.

She was going to leave.

Her hands were shaking. Strange, she thought. Her lungs ached with each cold breath she drew in. Leaving Brassmere. She was leaving Brassmere.

She reached the top of the gate and drew one leg over to the other side.

She paused. She wasn't sure what she had expected to happen. Some great explosion, perhaps, or for the world to end. In class she had been taught that the world outside Brassmere was not safe for exceptional people like herself. There were too many people who would try to trick her or cause her harm. There were liars and crooks and murderers. There were unspeakable things that happened every day, especially to children who were too trusting.

But all Plum saw were trees. Trees that were lush and thick and rustling on the cold breeze. Far in the distance, the twin gargoyles slept at either side of the entrance gate, a perfect match for the gold embroidered gargoyles on either sleeve of her coat. Plum had gone out of her way to avoid them; she'd heard rumors that they ate anyone who entered or left without their permission, and she most certainly did not have their permission.

Tentatively, she swung her other leg over the gate and began to descend. Climbing down the fence took more caution than going up, and so she moved slower. It didn't take much effort and she wasn't exerting herself, and still, her heart was racing as though she were running up a mountain full speed.

One boot touched the ground and then the other, and just like that, she was outside Brassmere. Here she paused, waiting for some great catastrophe to befall her. She had never been frightened to leave Brassmere—not exactly. It was more so that the idea of leaving Brassmere, *truly* leaving it, had not crossed her mind any more than flying across the clouds like a bird had crossed her mind. It was not allowed, nor had it seemed possible.

But now Plum suddenly felt as though anything was possible. It was exhilarating and strange, and she wasn't quite sure what to make of it.

She didn't feel that she had truly left Brassmere. Not yet. The school was still in sight. But the air smelled different. Burnt and crisp and even sweet. A smile spread across her mouth.

And then, she did what she had been instructed all her life never to do, something she had once believed would mean the end of the world:

She ran away.

CHAPTER 14

There was a road on the other side of the gate, and Plum ran alongside it at a distance for a while. There were no lights out here, and the trees obscured the moonlight, making everything dim.

Plum thought about Artem, who was terrified of the dark. She thought of him being carried along this road, deep asleep, an IV trailing from his arm.

It made her angry. She realized that now for the first time. Gentle, warm, kindhearted Artem who would never do a thing to harm anyone did not deserve to be ripped away from the only home he'd ever known.

She was angry with Dr. Abarrane especially, for being so much like a parent and then betraying them.

And she was confused. Why Artem? He was not the fastest, not the strongest, and by far not the bravest student at Brassmere. What was it about him that Dr. Abarrane needed?

Plum was still considering this when she came to a fork in the road. There were no signs, but from here, she could faintly hear the sound of something happening in the distance. She held her breath to listen.

It sounded like cars, she thought. The only cars she had ever seen or heard had been the ones driven by the pinks. The tires crunching over the gravel, the hum of the engine, and the rushing sound as they drove off, like a hard wind.

That sound was definitely cars. Maybe even

hundreds of them. There must have been a road to the left, then. A road meant people. It wasn't likely that Artem had gone somewhere with other people, Plum thought.

She took the path that forked to the right, where there were no sounds at all. In dreams, Artem was always seeking out these sorts of places: quiet and calm, with nothing growling or rustling in the grass. Plum was rather the opposite. If she knew there was a monster, she couldn't help but charge forward and conquer it. When she woke from those dreams, she always felt as though she had done something useful. The monsters always felt real somehow, even though they couldn't possibly be. Even though the world she woke up to had always been calm.

Perhaps it had been too calm, she thought now, as she moved ahead. Perhaps Artem's disappearance was not the only strange thing to have ever happened at Brassmere, but Dr. Abarrane had managed to hide it from her. She thought of how she spent her days: racing the other students on the track, or with her head bowed over her books as she studied, pen in hand. She was always focused. Always studious. But had that served to distract her from what was going on around her?

Artem did not obsess over things like running or studying; perhaps his anxiety came from his lack of distraction. He saw things as they really were. He was always watching.

What had he seen that Dr. Abarrane hadn't wanted him to?

A horrible fear lanced through her. The idea that he was in danger and that she should have known something was amiss long before it came to this.

Over and over again she reminded herself that she was awake. That this was real. When she looked over her shoulder, she couldn't see Brassmere. Its gargoyles had not eaten her when she made her escape.

It felt too easy, she thought. Too possible that

all she had to do to leave the only home she'd ever known was climb an iron gate.

There were no clocks out here in the forest beyond the gate. There was no sense of time. The trees obscured the stars. To remind herself that she was awake, Plum pressed her hand against the trees she passed. In dreams, the trees often bristled at her touch, or the bark produced a weapon, or the leaves were filled with magical flying little things.

Nothing extraordinary happened. Plum walked on.

And then, all at once, there was light in the form of windows on a building. It was the tallest building Plum had ever seen. She had to crane her neck to see the top of it.

You're not dreaming. To remind herself, she counted to ten in her head. Counting to ten was something she could only do when she was awake. Numbers and letters always eluded her in dreams.

She stepped closer, cautiously. The road came to an end at a giant concrete square before the building. It was unusual concrete, with little white lines painted onto it in the shape of rectangles with a missing side.

A map of some sort, perhaps. But the lines didn't seem to lead anywhere, and they stopped well before the door.

The door was wide, glass, and illuminated by the light within the building.

Plum didn't know what awaited her in this building, but she knew two things in that moment: Artem was inside, and she couldn't use the door. If Artem was here, she suspected that Dr. Abarrane was here as well, and that he would put her in that awful sleep again, from which she could not wake up.

No. There had to be another way in.

Keeping in the darkness of the trees, Plum circled the building and studied it. The first floor of the building was well lit. Then, remaining floors were all dark, except for the fourth floor, whose windows were glowing.

There.

She examined the trees. One of them ran alongside the building. Its branches reached toward one of the windows on the fourth floor, but they were thin, quaking on the breeze. Plum wasn't sure if they would hold her weight, but there was only one way to find out, and anyway she had no better options.

Halfway up the tree, she began to regret not waking Vien. Plum had strength and courage, but Vien always came up with a plan. He could look at anything as a puzzle and then figure out how to solve it.

But Vien was not here. He was in bed and dreaming of dangerous things that would all be gone by morning. Plum would have to figure this one out herself.

When she reached the fourth floor of the building, the branches that led to the window were even thinner up close. She held on to the tree's trunk, watching as the branches swayed back and forth like slender blades of grass.

She placed one tentative foot on a branch, and immediately it bent.

She looked down. There was nothing but grass below her. This building was not like the rock mountain in the training arena. There were no footholds.

The window had a ledge, about two feet deep. If the window were open, it would be an easy leap, Plum thought. But it was closed, and if she didn't land just right, there would be nothing to hold on to if she lost her balance.

Plum stood up straight, her feet rooted on one of the stable branches, and braced herself. Professor Nayamor would call this a poor decision, but Professor Nayamor did not have a friend inside that building. Professor Nayamor had not seen Artem, gaunt and frail and frightened, in her dreams. Professor Nayamor was not Artem's only hope.

She was.

Without taking another moment to think of the consequences, she jumped.

It was all her effort not to scream. She landed on the ledge and stumbled backward when the window blocked her momentum. *Don't panic.* She braced her hands on either side of the window's brick frame, steadying herself.

Her legs shook. Her heart was pounding. But she had made it. When she realized this, she laughed. She laughed at all her fear and her worry. She laughed at Dr. Abarrane for thinking he could stop her from reaching her friend.

The window took some effort to open, but Plum managed it, and then she slipped inside.

This was the exact same building as in her dream of the nursery. She knew it. It had the same strange smell, as though something sharp and abrasive had stripped the floor and walls and air of everything that indicated human life.

"Artem?" she whispered.

The room was a strange bedroom, with two empty beds framed by metal bars on either side, almost like the sides of a crib but only half as high. There was an empty cart, with an empty silver tray on the top. There were no closets and no other furniture at all. It felt very unsettling, as though all traces of whoever had slept here had been erased.

The door was open, and Plum cautiously stepped out into the hallway.

One, two, three, four, five, six, seven, eight, nine, ten. She counted more than once to be sure she wasn't dreaming, because this was exactly what she had dreamed earlier that night. She had dreamed a great number of things, but never anything that really existed.

She even counted the floor tiles as she walked. Her shoes echoed against the white marble tiles, and so she moved slowly, peeking into each doorway she passed. Room after room had empty beds and empty carts.

Voices from around the corner made her stop short.

". . . Patient has responded well to Treatment B,"

a woman was saying. "Tomorrow the doctor will want a full report of his vitals."

The voices were drawing closer, and Plum slid into an empty room. The door was ajar and she wedged herself behind it, keeping to the shadows and peeking through the crack between the door and the frame.

Two nurses walked briskly past. One of them glanced at her watch and said, "The doctor wants us to monitor him at the top of every hour."

Once they were gone, Plum crept back out into the hallway. The patient she'd overheard the nurse discussing must have been Artem, she thought. She hoped she was right. If Artem wasn't here, she would have to go back to the fork in the path and go the other way. The other way led to the world beyond the forest, and her professors said it went on and on forever. She didn't know how she would find Artem then.

There was a pattern of beeping sounds coming from one of the rooms. Her blood went cold when she heard it. The beeping was steady and slow.

She came upon the open doorway where the sound was coming from.

This room had the same cart and beds as the other rooms, but it wasn't empty. In one of the beds, there was a boy, fast asleep, one long tube trailing from his arm, and several thinner wires snaking out from under his collar and sleeves.

Artem.

CHAPTER 15

"A rtem!" Plum gasped.

Just as in their shared dream, Artem was pale and there were dark rings around his eyes. Even his curly brown hair seemed dull under the strange and too-bright lights.

She stood at his bedside, her hands hovering over the wires that kept him plugged into the machines. The wires that snaked out of his sleeves and collar were monitoring various parts of his chest. If she disconnected the machine from his heart, the machine would stop working.

Maybe the rhythmic beeps would turn into a sort of alarm and they would be caught.

The tube in his arm led to an IV that dripped in a bag over his bed. Plum recognized that odd purple liquid; it was the same thing Dr. Abarrane had given to her that morning when she couldn't sleep.

"I'm sorry, Artem," she murmured. "This might hurt a little."

She slid the IV needle out of his arm as carefully as she could. A drop of purple splattered on the white floor. A fat red circle of blood swelled on Artem's skin in the needle's absence.

Plum looked to the clock that hung above the door. The nurses would be back at the top of the hour to check on him, and that meant they had five minutes to escape.

"Artem." She shook his shoulder. *"Artem.* You have to wake up!"

It seemed like an eternity before Artem moved, even though it had only been a few seconds—Plum knew this because she was still glancing at the clock to prove that none of this was a dream.

First, his lashes fluttered. His hand twitched. And then, his eyes opened.

"Plum?" His voice was hoarse. "Are we in another dream?"

"No," she said. "No, this is real."

He looked confused at that, but then as his eyes began to sweep across the room, realization turned his expression fearful. The beeping on the monitor got a little faster. "The nurses," he rasped. "They brought me here. They made me sleep."

"I know," Plum said. She was doing her best not to sound as anxious as she felt; it would only frighten Artem more than he already was. "We have to go. Can you sit up?"

Artem pushed himself upright by his arms. The monitor beeped faster, and Plum frowned at what had to be done. Giving Artem no warning, she pulled at the wires trailing from his sleeves and collar. He let out a yelp of pain as the monitors came unstuck from his chest.

The machine let out a shrill, loud, flat beeping now that it no longer had a heart to measure.

Artem covered his ears. Plum grabbed his arm and tugged him to his feet. "Come on."

He wobbled unsteadily for a few steps, but by the time they reached the hallway, he was able to keep pace with her.

As footsteps came running down the hall, Artem was the one to latch on to Plum and pull them both into an empty bedroom.

"Where is the patient?" a nurse shouted.

"Calm down," another said. "He can't have gotten far."

Plum and Artem huddled together in the shadow behind the door, and Plum assessed their location.

How were they going to get out?

There was a window, but no tree to climb

down. They could listen for the nurses and run for the room by the tree Plum had used to climb in, but she worried about Artem. He had never done well with heights, and he might fall.

Something rumbled faintly in the ceiling, and a warm breeze of artificial air blew down on them, rustling their hair.

Plum looked up at the air vent.

"I've found our way out," she whispered.

It took some effort, but by locking the wheels on the empty cart, Plum was able to use it to shimmy the vent cover away from the ceiling and hoist herself inside.

Artem's legs were shaking slightly as he climbed onto the cart next. Plum grabbed his wrists. "I've got you," she said. "Brace your feet against the wall like you're walking. There. Like that."

With a final tug, she managed to pull him up beside her.

It wasn't a large air shaft, but there was room for both of them to kneel. As much as Plum wanted to keep moving, she could see that Artem was still dazed, and she felt guilty for pushing him so hard after all he'd been through.

He was still pale, but the color was coming slowly back to his cheeks.

"It feels like years ago," he said, "that you and I were lying on the back of that monster."

"That was tonight," Plum said. "Are you feeling all right now?" She nodded down the air shaft, to where there was a small rectangle of light bleeding upward from another vent. "If we follow the vents, we can find our way out."

Artem nodded, and he let Plum lead the way. They had to crawl. What Plum had never told anyone was that she hated small spaces. If this were a tightrope over a pit of boiling red lava, she would have felt better than she did now. But she said nothing. What Artem had just endured was worse, and for once, he wasn't allowing his fear of everything to best him. He was being quite brave, she thought.

They crawled for what felt like hours, until

Plum heard a muffled voice. She came to a stop, and Artem nearly crashed into her. "What is it?" he asked.

"Shh."

"If he woke himself, then he truly is the one we're looking for," a voice said.

Plum and Artem huddled over the air vent and peeked in on the room below them. This was not a bedroom. There was a computer and a steel table filled with odd metal instruments that looked almost like knives and needles.

Two people stood at either side of a metal table.

"Patient Number Four didn't wake himself." It was Dr. Abarrane. He sounded amused.

"Patient Number One?" the other person asked. It was the nurse Plum had seen earlier in the hallway.

"Yes," Dr. Abarrane said. "Plum. They can't have gotten far. He'll still be weak."

"What should we do?" the nurse asked.

From Plum's vantage point, she could see the smile on Dr. Abarrane's face. "We wait."

Plum didn't hesitate. She started crawling again, Artem at her heels.

"What did that mean?" Artem whispered.

"I don't know."

"Plum—"

"Just let me think," she said. When the air shaft came to a bend, she stopped. She was breathing hard, she realized. Not from adrenaline or fear, but from anger. Betrayal.

Patients. Dr. Abarrane had referred to them as patients.

It all came flashing through her mind at once—her imagined memories of Dr. Abarrane finding her on those church steps in a crate meant to hold plums. "It isn't true," she said. Artem knelt before her now, and she took his hands. "Artem, none of what we were told was ever true. I think—I think those things we dreamed were real. The man with the sheriff's badge and that city with the clock tower and—"

"The fire," Artem said. "Did you dream about a house that was on fire?"

"Yes," Plum said. "And a baby crying."

"That baby was probably one of us," Artem said. "Dr. Abarrane—" His expression twisted into a mix of confusion and sadness. "Were we even orphans, Plum? Did he take us from our parents?"

Plum thought of the woman she'd dreamed dead on the floor, surrounded by flames.

And then something very strange happened. Her vision blurred, and her cheeks felt wet, and she realized that she had begun to cry.

Plenty of students at Brassmere cried. Cried because they were injured, or sick, impatient, or sad. Cried because they were frustrated. Plum had seen it hundreds of times, but she had never understood the point. Why cry about something when you could fix it? But here, now, for the first time she had encountered something she could not fix. She could not put out the fire in that building she'd dreamed. Could not console the couple crying in that office. She could not bring that woman back from the dead.

She could not find her parents. And she could never, ever trust Dr. Abarrane again.

"Oh, Plum." Artem dabbed at her cheeks with the sleeve of his medical gown. "Don't do that. Don't cry. We'll find a way out."

"I know that." Plum sniffled. "But then where will we go?"

CHAPTER 16

Plum did not allow herself to cry for long. Artem tried to give her a hug, but she brushed him off. Somehow she knew that this would only make her cry more. There was something so sad about kindness sometimes.

"We need to move," she said instead. "We have to get back to Gwendle and Vien and tell them."

"We have to tell everyone," Artem said as they resumed their crawl. "They have a right to know."

"I don't think they'll believe us," Plum said. She barely believed it herself. But this building was proof that some of the things she dreamed had been real. It was like there was a map of this place in her head, as though it had been whispered to her while she was sleeping one night and she'd retained it.

She thought of the pinks, who monitored her pulse and took her blood. Is that all they were? Patients? Experiments?

Plum stopped them at a vent that overlooked a stairwell. This was probably going to be their only way out, she thought.

"Do you feel well enough to jump?" she asked Artem. Her voice was still tight with her spent tears, but Artem was kind enough not to notice.

"Yes," he said. "But won't we be caught?"

"Maybe not," Plum said. "I saw the building from the outside, and none of the other floors had any lights. I think we can sneak down to the second floor, then we'll be close enough to the ground to climb down from one of the smaller trees."

Artem smiled for the first time in what felt like forever. "You've got this all figured out."

Plum didn't have anything figured out. Her entire world was spinning. But dwelling on it wouldn't help. She worked the vent cover up. Then she braced her hands on the edge and jumped down.

She landed hard, bending her knees to absorb the blow.

Artem came after her, and he only stumbled a little bit, steadied when she grabbed his arm.

The rest of the escape went exactly as Plum had planned, which Plum found unusual. As they climbed down the tree and made their way back into the forest, Dr. Abarrane's words echoed in her head:

We wait.

What did that mean? What did any of this mean?

Artem stopped running, and Plum thought he might be hurt. But when she turned to face him, she saw that he was staring at the building from which they'd just escaped. And then he was staring at the forest that surrounded it.

"Are we . . . outside the fence?" he asked.

"It's big out here, isn't it?" Plum said.

He was shivering. All he had to wear was a thin gown that did nothing against the autumn chill. Plum shrugged out of her coat and draped it over his shoulders.

"Come on," she said. "We have to get back to Vien and Gwendle."

Plum would have liked to run. She could have run. But Artem was still weak, and Plum felt guilty for pushing him so much. He'd just spent three days trapped in a coma, unable to escape the loneliness of his dreams, and here she was making him run through a strange forest in the middle of the night.

They had to stop several times, and when

they did, Plum huddled under the coat beside Artem to keep warm.

"I'm sorry," he said, his teeth chattering from the cold. "I'm slowing us down."

"It's not your fault," Plum said. "It's Dr. Abarrane's fault. All of this is his fault."

She felt a surge of anger at his name, but that was a good thing. Anger motivated her to keep going.

By the time they reached the iron fence that surrounded Brassmere, the sky had begun to turn pale, and soon the sun would rise. Birds flitted in the trees, cheerily making music as they went about their business.

Artem marveled that they were standing on the wrong side of the fence. The twin gargoyles sat stoic on either side of the entrance, and Artem extended his hand high above his head so that he could touch one of their talons.

"They're not really alive?" he asked, and laughed. "All this time, I've been so frightened of even getting *close* to the gate. I was so sure they would eat me."

"They're not alive," Plum affirmed. "That was a lie."

She was going to say something else, but an odd sound of stone grating against stone made her fall silent. She looked up at the gargoyle Artem was touching.

The gargoyle turned its head toward her.

And then, it lunged.

CHAPTER 17

Artem grabbed Plum's arm and pulled her roughly toward him. The spot where she had been standing was a mound of ruined dirt where the gargoyle had attacked.

The other gargoyle sprang to life, too, and Plum's mind was spinning to understand. She hadn't slept for hours, and she was exhausted. *Focus*, she scolded herself, and tried to stay sharp.

She braced herself for another attack, but the gargoyle didn't come after her again. The gargoyles' stone bodies transformed rapidly into leathery gray flesh, and they leaped into the air in tandem, their giant wings spreading out as they took flight.

"They're heading for the school!" Artem cried. One of the gargoyles was barreling through the overarching glass window of the grand foyer. The other had scaled the side of the building that housed the dormitory, and its giant swinging tail was shattering the windows.

Plum and Artem climbed the gate in tandem. Despite his fear of heights, Artem did a good job keeping up with Plum. While they were climbing, at least. Going down was a different story. For once, Artem kept his fears to himself, but Plum could see that he was trembling. She slowed her own pace to keep time with him, and when they reached the ground, she said, "Are you okay?"

He nodded. "Let's go."

They ran and entered Brassmere through the mess of glass and splintered wood. It wasn't only the gargoyles that had come to life. All the birds and insects in the wallpaper had escaped and were buzzing and flapping at the ceiling and remaining windows, trying to find a way out. The carved owls had broken free of the clock hands, and one of them was pecking at a student's hair as he swatted at it, screaming.

Students had come out of their dorms now, awoken by the commotion.

At the heart of it all stood Melinda. She was in the center of the foyer, her eyes hollow and dazed as they had been the other night. Before her, the piano churned out a low and dangerous melody. It only added to the frenzied chaos of the newly animated things and the students rushing past.

The students poured out of the building, racing past Plum and Artem and Melinda, bumping their shoulders as they went.

"Plum!" Vien was the first to spot them, and then Gwendle was right behind him. "Artem!"

Gwendle threw her arms around them both. "You found him!" She took Artem's face in her hands. "You're okay."

Artem was still watching Melinda, who was working the metal wires of the piano, her face unmoving. "I'm not sure any of us are okay."

Plum could see in Vien's eyes that he had questions but there was no time to ask them in all this uproar.

"Is this a dream?" Gwendle asked.

"I wish," Plum said. The school seemed to be crumbling all around them, but she had stopped counting to ten in her head. She had learned in the past several hours that reality could be just as strange as her wildest dreams.

They were the only students left at Brassmere now. Even Melinda's three partners had fled, one of them screaming for her to stop as she raced past. It occurred to Plum now that she, Vien, Artem, and Gwendle were the only ones brave enough for this. In an academy of exceptional students with extraordinary abilities, years of battling monsters in dreams meant that those four were the only ones willing to face this particular nightmare.

Overhead, the insects and birds were still screeching and fluttering into and around one another. One of the gargoyles was destroying the side of the building with his tail, while they could hear the other stomping about somewhere on the roof. When the music hit a rift, the chaos seemed to intensify.

"The gargoyles didn't come to life on their own," Plum realized aloud. "It's the music. The music is doing it."

"Melinda," Gwendle cried. "You have to stop."

Plum moved closer, until she was standing face-to-face with Melinda. "Look at me." She had to shout over the music. "You're asleep. You have to wake up."

The music went on.

"Melinda!" Plum grabbed her shoulders.

When they touched, the music came to a sudden halt. Melinda raised her head and looked at Plum, her mouth curled into a vicious snarl.

And then, Plum was airborne, flying backward by the metal in her boot buckles and the buttons of her coat, until she hit a wall, hard, and everything went dark.

CHAPTER 18

In the dream, Plum could hear Vien's scream the loudest. She tasted blood on her tongue.

She wasn't all the way asleep. She could still feel a little bit of reality trying to steal its way in. She felt her bones, all broken and shaking loose in her skin. She saw the birds and owls and gargoyles flying overhead in the blood red sky of her dream.

The piano music had stopped, though, and everything was quiet.

"Plum?" Vien's voice echoed.

She couldn't answer him. She couldn't move. Even in her dream, her entire body was broken.

CHAPTER 19

In this part of the dream, Plum no longer had a body. All she had were eyes and ears. All she could do was watch and listen.

She saw the beautiful woman with the short dark hair from her earlier dreams. She was alive again now, holding a baby on her hip. The baby looked quite a bit like her, with dark hair and eyes and round cheeks.

There was a man standing beside her. He was the same man Plum had dreamed earlier, only this time he wasn't wearing a pinstriped suit. He was wearing a crisply pressed white button-up shirt with a tie, and starched gray pants, and perfectly polished shoes.

It took a moment for the background to materialize behind them. And then Plum realized, with dread, that they were standing in a room of the very same building from which she and Artem had escaped.

"Is a hospital really necessary?" the woman asked. *Hospital.* The word was new to Plum. She knew there were all sorts of buildings outside Brassmere, but she hadn't known that they had their own names.

A man materialized before the couple and their baby. Dr. Abarrane. He looked young, just as he had in Plum's earlier dream. He held out his arms for the baby. "May I?"

Hesitantly, the woman handed the baby over, and Dr. Abarrane hoisted her into his arms, weighing her and assessing her as he so often did with all his students. "You said that she has trouble with sleeping ever since her first treatment."

"Not trouble sleeping," the man said. "She has no trouble sleeping. The problem is that she sleeps all the time. All night and sometimes even all day. More than once we've thought she was dead."

Dr. Abarrane set the baby on the bed. She was just old enough to sit upright, and she giggled and kicked her feet at him.

"She seems perfectly awake right now," he said. "Have any of the other children responded to their treatment this way?"

"Three of them," the woman said. "Another girl and two of the boys." She looked horribly worried.

"But she seems the most affected," the man said.

Dr. Abarrane crouched before the baby, shining a flashlight in her ears and down her throat. "I wouldn't worry," he said. "The serums will have side effects, but that's a small price to pay for these children not to be taken down by the Red Flu."

The dream faded.

The next dream came fast in its place, filled with fire and ash and screaming. Plum watched on, powerless, unable to move, unable to do anything but look as she once again saw the burning house.

There was a room filled with at least a dozen cribs, all of which were empty now except for one. The baby from the first part of the dream was standing, trying to climb over the bars as smoke blackened her view. She was going to do it, too, Plum could see. She was quite a determined little thing. But the woman came running in and scooped her up before she could make it all the way.

Coughing and running, the woman hurried the baby down a staircase. The room at the bottom was engulfed in flames, but there was still a path. There was still a chance.

The woman ran for the door. The baby was wriggling in her arms, as though she had a better escape plan.

But it wouldn't have mattered if she did. The door swung open, and there stood the young Dr. Abarrane. Something was in his hands. It was a weapon. Plum knew that much. But she had never seen one like it before. It had a barrel and a trigger of some sort, but there were no blades. Maybe the blade was hidden, and pulling the trigger would release it.

Whatever the weapon was, the woman recognized it. Fear filled her eyes. She hugged the baby against her, shielding her head with her hand. "No," she said. "You aren't going to take her from me. Not this one. Not my own."

Dr. Abarrane didn't bother to argue. He pulled the trigger, and before Plum even had time to see what was happening, the woman had fallen to the ground. Dead.

The baby screamed and fell into a fit of tears. Dr. Abarrane picked her up and whisked her outside. He didn't bother to comfort her. He just ran.

Plum dreamed on. The dream turned feverish after that. They were back at the hospital. There was a room filled with cradles and babies, many of them with ash and soot in their hair and on their cheeks. There were nurses wiping their faces and comforting them and offering them bottles of juice or milk.

Dr. Abarrane sat in a chair, comforting the baby he had taken from the burning house himself. The baby was calmer now, staring back at him as she drank from the bottle in his hand.

"It's all right now," he said. "You're home now, Plum."

CHAPTER 20

When Plum opened her eyes, this time she knew that she was awake. She knew, because the first thing she saw was a clock ticking above the door to an all-white room that smelled of strange chemicals.

Her heart sank.

She was back in the hospital she'd escaped with Artem.

Where was Artem? Where were Vien and Gwendle? Around her, the room was empty. There was a window, but she could see from her bed that it had been nailed shut. It was dark out again, which meant that Plum had been asleep for at least a day.

Her ribs and head ached, and she tried to push herself upright, but she could hardly move.

Dully, she remembered Melinda at the piano. The wicked look in her eyes. And then, being thrown back.

Again she tried to sit upright, and this time she managed it, biting hard on her lower lip to stifle her cry of pain.

There was an IV stuck in her left arm, and slowly, carefully, she pulled it out. Blood welled up in the spot.

The door opened, and there stood Dr. Abarrane. He was smiling, and he brought his hands together in a clap, and then another.

"Well done, Plum," he said. "I was impressed by your escape, but then, I shouldn't have been. You've exceeded my expectations right from the start."

Her head felt as though her skull had been cracked open. She was tired and sore. But more than that, she was angry. Her jaw swelled with all her anger. For the first time in her life, she understood what hatred was. She hated Dr. Abarrane.

"Was it true?" she asked.

He pulled up a chair and sat by her bed. "Was what true?" He seemed fascinated, as though she were a specimen under a microscope for him to examine. "What is it you dreamed, Plum?"

Plum told him exactly what she had seen, the hospital and the boy who died and the burning house. But whatever reaction she might have expected from Dr. Abarrane, he didn't give it. He only smiled, like he was proud of her.

"You have always exceeded my expectations." He echoed his earlier sentiment.

"Who was that woman you killed?" Plum demanded.

"You mean you haven't figured that out?" Dr.

Abarrane said, as though it should be obvious. "Plum, that was the woman who gave birth to you."

Plum's anger went wild. She forgot her pain and jumped out of the bed.

Dr. Abarrane didn't try to stop her.

"Why?" Her voice was a gasp. She was normally so good at controlling her emotions, at not being upset, at letting logic and practicality prevail. But not now. She had never had a mother before, and it stirred a torrent of feelings she never knew she was capable of having within her. "Why did you kill her?"

"She had fulfilled her use to me," Dr. Abarrane said. He nodded to the bed. "Please, sit. There's no need to be hysterical. I'll explain everything."

Plum did not sit. He went on nonetheless.

"The year that you were born, several thousand children all across the country died of what came to be known as the Red Flu. I was the one to develop the vaccination. You were among my very first test patients, and the results were successful, but there was a happy and unexpected side effect. Several of the children to receive this vaccine developed extraordinary gifts. You can't do it anymore, but when you were a baby, objects would float over your cradle as you slept. Eventually it turned into tandem dreaming with three other subjects."

Three other subjects. Vien, Gwendle, and Artem.

"Your parents were ordinary," Dr. Abarrane said. "They couldn't know how to handle such precious gifts. They didn't deserve to raise you."

Plum stumbled back, toward the door.

Dr. Abarrane stood to go after her. "Don't you get it? At Brassmere you've learned to be the best of the best. Your ability to dream gets stronger every day. You've begun even dreaming of real things that happened in the past, things you couldn't have possibly remembered on your own."

Plum shook her head. For the first time in her life, she didn't want her extraordinary gift. She didn't want to be exceptional. All those years of being the fastest runner and the sharpest reader and the coolest head in a frenzy—all of it had been at the cost of having a family. Her mother and father died for it. It wasn't worth it, not a single moment of it.

"I've been watching your progress this week," Dr. Abarrane said. "I suspected you would come after Artem and that you would think to use the vents. There were cameras on you the whole time. It was astonishing to watch."

Plum was hardly listening to him now, her mind was racing so loudly through her ears.

She wished she were ordinary. She wished she were in a normal house with her normal mother and father, and that each morning she awoke from normal dreams.

Dr. Abarrane reached for her, and she ran. She ran down the hall, shouting for Vien and Artem and Gwendle.

She ran until she reached the stairwell, and

she pulled on the door handle. It didn't budge. Locked.

Dr. Abarrane was coming for her, and Plum realized now that she had cornered herself here in the hallway. He was still smiling, a syringe in his hand. "It's going to be all right," he said. "Nobody is going to hurt you. You're going to rest now, and you'll feel better—"

He didn't have time to finish the sentence before a metal tray hit him in the side of the head, hard. All it took was one blow and he was down. When he fell, Plum saw Vien standing with the tray in his hands. He was pale and gasping, blood leaking from his arm.

He gave Plum a weary grin. "All that talk of how exceptional we are," he panted, "and Dr. Abarrane still underestimates us."

Gwendle and Artem were easy to find. And then, wrapped in hospital blankets, the four of them made their escape into the cold night air.

When they reached the fork in the road, Plum

could once again hear the cars and the signs of life outside Brassmere.

Tired and holding one another up for support, they trudged on.

The path went on for so long that the sun was once again starting to rise when they finally reached the end of the woods.

"Where do you suppose the others are?" Gwendle asked, the first to speak in a long while.

"What happened to them after I blacked out?" Plum asked.

"I don't remember much," Gwendle said.

"They ran into the forest," Vien said.

"They probably went back to Brassmere," Artem said. "Even if the building was starting to fall apart. It's cold out, and that's the only home they know."

The road rose at a sharp incline, and they were all dragging their feet now.

"We'll come back for them," Vien said, reassuring Plum, whose guilt he could read. "We have to find help. We can't do anything for them on our own."

Plum gave him a weary, grateful smile.

The sound of traffic had grown louder now. They walked in silence, until they finally reached the top of the hill, where their road snaked out into another road, this one filled with cars. They gasped at the sight of them.

Beyond the roads, over the trees, the sun was rising over a brand-new day.

EPILOGUE

There were no monsters in this dream.

At first, there was the night sky and its smattering of stars. Then, gradually, the silhouette of a mountain appeared in the distance. Then crickets, blades of grass, and Plum, who was so often the first to arrive.

She heard Vien's approach. He wasn't quiet about treading through the rocks and the gravel path that appeared below his feet as he moved.

Plum spun to face him. He was not entirely the same as she remembered. Taller now, and willowy, with thin silver-rimmed glasses and hair that had grown long enough to be tied back into a neat ponytail.

He smiled when he saw her. "You remembered."

"I always remember your birthday," Plum said, pretending to take offense. This had become their ritual in the five years since they'd left Brassmere and found their true families. Plum lived with an aunt in a house that wasn't very far from the forest that once held Brassmere. It was a lovely sort of cottage with window boxes filled with red roses. But even better were the stories Plum's aunt told her of the parents Plum never got to know. There were hundreds of stories. Thousands. Enough to fill all the shelves in the library. And there were photographs of a woman with Plum's dark, confident eyes, and a man with her same smile—sly and toothy, like he was about to give up a secret.

Still, these stories did leave Plum with an

aching in her chest. Of all the things Dr. Abarrane had cost her, this loss was the greatest.

Though Brassmere had once been Plum's entire life, it was never spoken of again as she grew, though it was often in her thoughts.

Gwendle and Artem were reunited with their parents in other parts of the country entirely. But Vien, it turned out, was the son of world travelers who had been looking for him his entire life. Vien often entered his friends' tandem dreams, bringing them dreams of Paris or Spain, or the rainbow patterns of the northern lights, like a silk scarf swimming in the stars.

Even though there was distance between the four of them now, their tandem dreams held strong. They had all learned to control them better, though, and there were rarely monsters anymore. Plum had even learned how to build walls around her mind and sometimes dream alone.

But the four of them had always vowed to dream in tandem on important occasions, such as the anniversary of their escape from Brass-mere, or birthdays. Gwendle and Artem would be along eventually, stirring the clouds with their laughter and filling the dream with bright and happy energy.

But Plum and Vien had a vow of their own. They met early and talked about their lives. About the day they would meet again. Happy things, mostly. Sometimes sad. But always honest.

They stood on a mossy cliff side now, and Vien had painted an ocean below them. It sparkled like millions of stars.

The waking world was nowhere to be seen.